MELVIN BEEDERMAN SUPERHERO

BOOK 1: THE CURSE OF THE BOLOGNA SANDWICH

In which superhero Melvin Beederman and third-grader Candace Brinkwater team up to stop bad guys in Los Angeles.

BOOK 2: THE REVENGE OF THE McNASTY BROTHERS

In which the McNasty Brothers escape from prison to get revenge on Melvin and his partner in uncrime, Candace.

BOOK 3: THE GRATEFUL FRED

In which Melvin and Candace must find who is out to get rock star Fred of The Grateful Fred.

Coming Soon:

BOOK 4: DOOM WITH A VIEW

THE REVENGE OF THE McNASTY BROTHERS

GREG TRINE

ILLUSTRATED BY
RHODE MONTIJO

HENRY HOLT AND COMPANY ★ NEW YORK

For Lindsay and Amy
—*G. T.*

For my brother Ivan
—*R. M.*

Henry Holt and Company, LLC
Publishers since 1866
175 Fifth Avenue, New York, New York 10010
www.henryholtchildrensbooks.com

Henry Holt® is a registered trademark of Henry Holt and Company, LLC.
Text copyright © 2006 by Greg Trine
Illustrations copyright © 2006 by Rhode Montijo
All rights reserved.
Distributed in Canada by H. B. Fenn and Company Ltd.

Library of Congress Cataloging-in-Publication Data
Trine, Greg.
The revenge of the McNasty brothers /
Greg Trine ; illustrated by Rhode Montijo.—1st hardcover and paperback eds.
p.   cm.— (Melvin Beederman, superhero)
title: Revenge of the McNasty brothers.
Summary: As Melvin and Candace continue their crime-fighting work
as superheroes, the McNasty Brothers, the McNasty Sisters,
and the school bullies all plot to get even with them.
ISBN-13: 978-0-8050-7929-6 / ISBN-10: 0-8050-7929-7 (hardcover)
1   3   5   7   9   10   8   6   4   2

ISBN-13: 978-0-8050-7837-4 / ISBN-10: 0-8050-7837-1 (paperback)
1   3   5   7   9   10   8   6   4   2

[1. Heroes–Fiction. 2. Humorous stories.]
I. Montijo, Rhode, ill. II. Title. III. Series.
PZ7.T7356Re 2006   [Fic]—dc22   2005013999
First Edition—2006
Hand-lettering by David Gatti
Book designed by Donna Mark and Laurent Linn
Printed in the United States of America on acid-free paper. ∞

CONTENTS

THE INTRUDER

Superhero Melvin Beederman lived in a tree house overlooking Los Angeles, California. When he wasn't catching bad guys or rescuing good guys, he was home in his tree, watching cartoons.

And eating pretzels.

And drinking root beer.

And doing math problems during commercials.

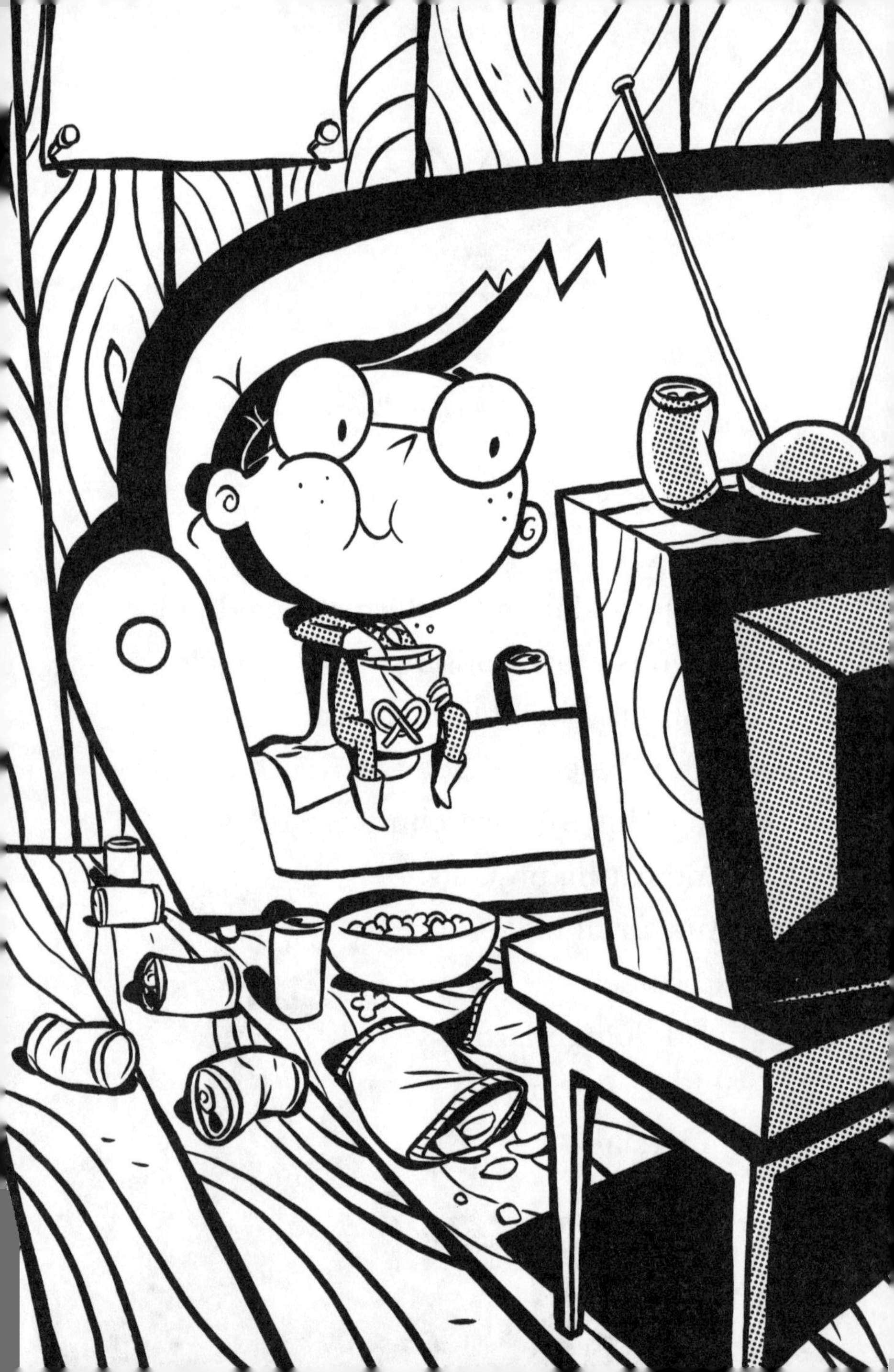

This is what superheroes do when they're not working. The only thing that changes is the snack . . . and the math. Why was Melvin taking it so easy? Because the McNasty Brothers, those notorious bank robbers and all-around bad guys, were back in prison where they belonged. There were other bad guys who needed catching, of course. But they were not nearly as nasty as the McNasty Brothers.

They didn't smell as bad either.

So Melvin was taking a break and watching his favorite show, *The Adventures of Thunderman*. Like most superheroes, Thunderman had an assistant. Her name was Thunder Thighs. Melvin Beederman also had an assistant—

Candace Brinkwater. The only person ever to run the hundred-yard dash in three and a half seconds. The only person ever to score 500 points in a basketball game. The only third-grader who could fly.

This flying stuff came in pretty handy for a superhero.

When *The Adventures of Thunderman* was over, Melvin typed an e-mail to his assistant.

Dear Candace,

Meet me at the library after school.
We'll do a little math, then catch some bad guys.

Sincerely,
Your partner in uncrime,
Melvin

This was their agreement: Melvin helped Candace with math, and she helped him save the world. Candace's parents loved having a daughter who saved the world on a regular basis—just as long as she was home for dinner.

Melvin pressed SEND on his computer. Suddenly, he heard something.

Squeak squeak.

Melvin jumped to his feet. He wasn't alone. "Who's there?"

Squeak squeak.

The squeaking was coming from behind the TV.

Melvin got ready to fight. "Whoever you are, come out with your hands up."

Wait a minute. That was policeman talk. And Melvin was a superhero, not a policeman. The squeaking intruder must have caught him off guard. He couldn't think.

"Come out and show yourself." *That's more like it,* Melvin thought. Superhero lingo. He'd learned the lingo along with the Superhero's Code at the academy. Years ago, he'd been plucked from an orphanage and sent there. And now he was on his own in Los Angeles, his first job since graduating. His tree house was his superhero's hideout—but maybe he wasn't as alone as he thought.

Squeak squeak.

He grabbed the TV and pushed it aside. Even though he stopped trains and outran bullets for a living, his heart was pounding.

Squeak squeak.

Melvin stared with his mouth open.

The intruder was nothing but a rat. A big rat, but a rat.

Melvin and the rat looked at each other. The rat wiggled his whiskers. Melvin didn't have whiskers to wiggle. He wiggled his eyebrows instead.

"Hit the road, rat," Melvin said.

The rat didn't move.

"Take off. Scat. Beat it."

The rat stayed.

"Get out of—" Melvin stopped. Back at the Superhero Academy he could speak gerbil. And this rat was kind of like a gerbil. Four legs. A tail. Fur.

Melvin gave his eyebrows another wiggle. This was part of gerbil language. If he had whiskers he'd give them a shake. But eyebrows were all he had to work with. Then he said, "Squeak."

The rat looked startled. "Squeak?"

"Squeak squeak." Melvin kept those eyebrows wiggling.

The rat did likewise with his whiskers. "Squeak squeak?"

"Squeak squeak squeak." Melvin wasn't sure, but he thought he'd just said, "Do you like pretzels?" or possibly, "What's your favorite Thunderman episode?"

Melvin held out a pretzel. The rat

came forward and sniffed. Then he took it in his teeth and backed away. Melvin turned the TV back on and gave the rat another pretzel.

Before long the two of them were watching TV together. And eating pretzels. *If only this rat was good at math,* Melvin thought.

It was too much to hope for, of course. But for now Melvin had a pet. He named him Hugo.

Later that day, Melvin was trying to get off the ground.

"Up, up, and away." *Crash!*

"Up, up, and away." *Splat!*

It always took him many tries to get up and flying. But this time it didn't bother him.

"Wait till Candace Brinkwater hears about this," he said to himself. "I have a roommate!"

TWO AGAINST ONE

Now that she was a superhero, Candace Brinkwater no longer rode the bus to school. She flew. She put on her cape and flew.

Candace had first come across the cape after a mix-up at the dry cleaners. Melvin got her cape by mistake. She got his. And with it came the power to fly, the power to stop trains. In the end, Melvin divided the cape with her. Two superheroes are better than one, as they say. And Los Angeles was better off because of it.

So now when it was time for school, she just yelled, "Up, up, and away."

And she always got off the ground on the first try. Always.

Once at school, she kept on her cape. She had to. There were kickball games to play during recess. There were basketballs that needed to be slam-dunked. And there was also the chance she could break her own world record in the hundred-yard dash—three and a half seconds.

Mostly she kept on her cape so that kids would behave themselves. When Candace Brinkwater was around, bullies watched their step.

Candace had once showed up just in the nick of time to catch a couple of milk money thieves. They were the school's biggest bullies, Johnny Fink and Knucklehead Wilson. Everybody thought Knucklehead was the leader, but it was really Johnny.

Johnny came from a long line of bullies. His father was a bully. His mother was a bully. Even his goldfish was a bully. If you put your finger in their fishbowl, you'd better be prepared to be picked on. Bullying was their family tradition. And it had been going on for years.

It was the same with Knucklehead Wilson's family. Bullies, every last one of them.

"School's no fun anymore," Johnny complained to Knucklehead. They were sitting together at recess. All the other kids were busy playing. But not these two.

"I know," said Knucklehead.

"I haven't picked on anybody all week."

"I know," said Knucklehead. He didn't talk much, but he was an expert at saying "I know."

"Something has to be done about Candace Brinkwater."

Johnny and Knucklehead looked across the school yard at Candace, who was busy slam-dunking a basketball, red cape flapping behind her.

"I miss bullying," Johnny said. "I really do."

"I know," said Knucklehead.

The two boys walked over to the basketball court where Candace was playing.

"Why don't you leave your cape at home, Candace?" Johnny asked.

Candace stopped in midair just below the basket. She didn't slam the ball. She just looked at Johnny and Knucklehead, trying to ignore their underwear. "You don't know what you're asking. If I left my cape at home, this school would be a different place."

"Exactly," said Johnny.

"We know," said Knucklehead.

Candace landed lightly on the ground and walked over, holding the ball on her hip. "You two up for a game?" she asked. "Two against one. I won't even slam-dunk. If you win I'll leave my cape at home."

Johnny and Knucklehead put their heads together. They talked it over. Two on one against Candace Brinkwater? The girl who scored 500 points in one game? The girl who ran the hundred-yard dash in three and a half seconds? The girl who could fly?

On the other hand, they really did miss bullying.

It was worth a try.

Johnny grabbed the ball from Candace. "Deal," he said. "If we win, you leave your cape at home." He passed the ball to Knucklehead, who dribbled it up-court and laid it in the basket for two points.

Candace wasn't worried. This was part of her plan.

"Make it, take it?" Johnny asked.

"Yes, if you make it, you keep the ball."

Johnny inbounded the ball again, but this time Candace was on Knucklehead like stink on a skunk, like cheese on a pizza . . . like a superhero on a bad guy.

When Knucklehead pulled up to shoot, she swatted the ball away. She grabbed it and passed it the full length of the court, then zoomed to the other end, caught it, and tossed it in.

"Make it, take it?" she said with a smile.

"Yes," Johnny said. He knew he had been tricked.

And Candace was glad to have done the tricking. Once she got the ball, there was no giving it up. She inbounded the ball to herself, then ran to catch it, and scored again.

She didn't need to slam-dunk. She just needed to run fast.

And she did run fast—very fast.

First she passed crosscourt to herself. *Swish*. Then she bounce-passed to herself. *Swish*.

Johnny and Knucklehead tried to block her. They tried to tackle her.

Nothing worked. Candace was too fast for them.

She shot from the outside. *Swish.* She shot in close. *Swish.* She got every rebound.

Johnny and Knucklehead dove at her from opposite sides of the court. But Candace moved, and the two boys ended up hugging in center court. "Hope nobody saw that," Johnny whispered.

Of course everybody had. A crowd had gathered and began cheering, "Go, Candace, go." The school wimps and geeks were glad to see Johnny and Knucklehead get a beating, even if it was only in a game of basketball. "Candace, you're the greatest!"

By the time the bell rang she was ahead by 96 points. This was pretty good, considering she didn't slam-dunk a single ball.

Candace shook hands with the boys. "Great game. Care for a rematch?"

"We'll think about it."

Johnny Fink and Knucklehead Wilson walked away.

"I hate Candace Brinkwater," Johnny said.

Knucklehead nodded. "I know."

I HATE BEEDERMAN.
HOW ABOUT YOU?

While Melvin Beederman was getting to know his new roommate, Hugo, and Candace Brinkwater was busy keeping the bullies in line at school, all was not well at the county prison.

This was where Filthy McNasty and his brother, Grunge, were. Everybody thought Filthy was the leader, but it was really Grunge. Grunge McNasty was locked up on the west side of the prison. Filthy was locked up on the east side. The guards never let brothers share the same prison cell—especially notorious bank robbers and all-around bad guys.

Now that they were locked up, they had nothing to do but think about Melvin Beederman. And think about him they did. Day and night they did nothing but think of him . . . and plot revenge.

Finally Grunge had had enough with thinking. He went to the bars of his cell

and began to chant. "I hate Beederman, yes, I do. I hate Beederman. How about you?"

There was a pause. Then a voice came back. "I hate Beederman, yes, I do. I hate Beederman. How about you?" It was Filthy McNasty, of course.

It went back and forth—Grunge chanted, and Filthy chanted in return. Each time it got louder. Pretty soon the whole prison joined in. The inmates on the west side of the prison didn't want to be outdone by the inmates on the east side. Most of them didn't even know who Melvin Beederman was. But that didn't stop them from yelling.

"We hate Beederman, yes, we do. We hate Beederman. How about you?"

Later, Grunge McNasty paced up and down in his cell. "Melvin Beederman," he said, "I'm going to get you." He stopped pacing and thought for a moment. "If only you couldn't run so fast. If only you couldn't fly. If only you couldn't see my underwear."

On the other side of the prison, Filthy McNasty was thinking the same thing. He hated that Melvin Beederman could see his underwear.

MEANWHILE . . .

At that very moment, two women were tunneling under the prison. They had shovels in their hands and flashlights strapped to their heads. These were the McNasty Sisters, Mudball McNasty and

her sister, Puke—notorious jewel thieves and all-around bad girls. Everybody thought Mudball was the leader, but it was really Puke.

"Keep working, Mudball," Puke said.

"Anything you say, Puke." Mudball stopped shoveling and turned to her sister. "Why are we doing this again?"

"We're breaking our brothers out of prison."

Mudball scratched her head. "Who are they again?"

"Filthy and Grunge, put in prison by

Melvin Beederman and his superhero assistant."

"Yes. Of course. Exactly." It sometimes took a while, but Mudball caught on eventually.

The two sisters dug and dug and dug.

Finally they stopped, and Puke pulled out the map of the prison. "Grunge is locked up on the west side. I think we're getting close." It was Puke's plan to rescue Grunge first, since he was the leader of the McNasty Brothers, those notorious . . . well, you know the rest.

"Grunge?" Mudball asked.

"Your brother."

"Yes. Of course. Exactly."

They kept digging, but stopped when they heard something.

Mudball sniffed. "Do you hear something?"

"Sounds like voices," Puke said. "Some kind of chanting."

They began to dig at the ceiling of the tunnel. "We must be under the prison. Listen."

The chanting was very soft, but it grew louder as the two sisters cleared away more dirt from the ceiling.

"What are they saying?" Mudball asked. "What's a Beederman?"

"Melvin Beederman. Superhero, cape, x-ray vision. Ringing any bells, Mudball?"

"Oh, Beederman. Yes. Of course. Exactly. We're almost there, Puke. Keep digging."

"Hey, I'm the leader here, and don't you forget it!" Puke said.

"Okay," Mudball agreed.

"We're almost there, Mudball. Keep digging."

They did.

They dug.

Right through the floor of the prison.

Above them they heard, "I hate Beederman, yes, I do. I hate Beederman. How about—"

Crash! A hole suddenly appeared in the floor of Grunge McNasty's prison cell, and he fell through it.

"—YOU!" he yelled. He hated leaving sentences unfinished.

He stood up. "What in tarnation!" Then he saw his sisters and smiled. "You two are a sore for sight eyes. I mean—"

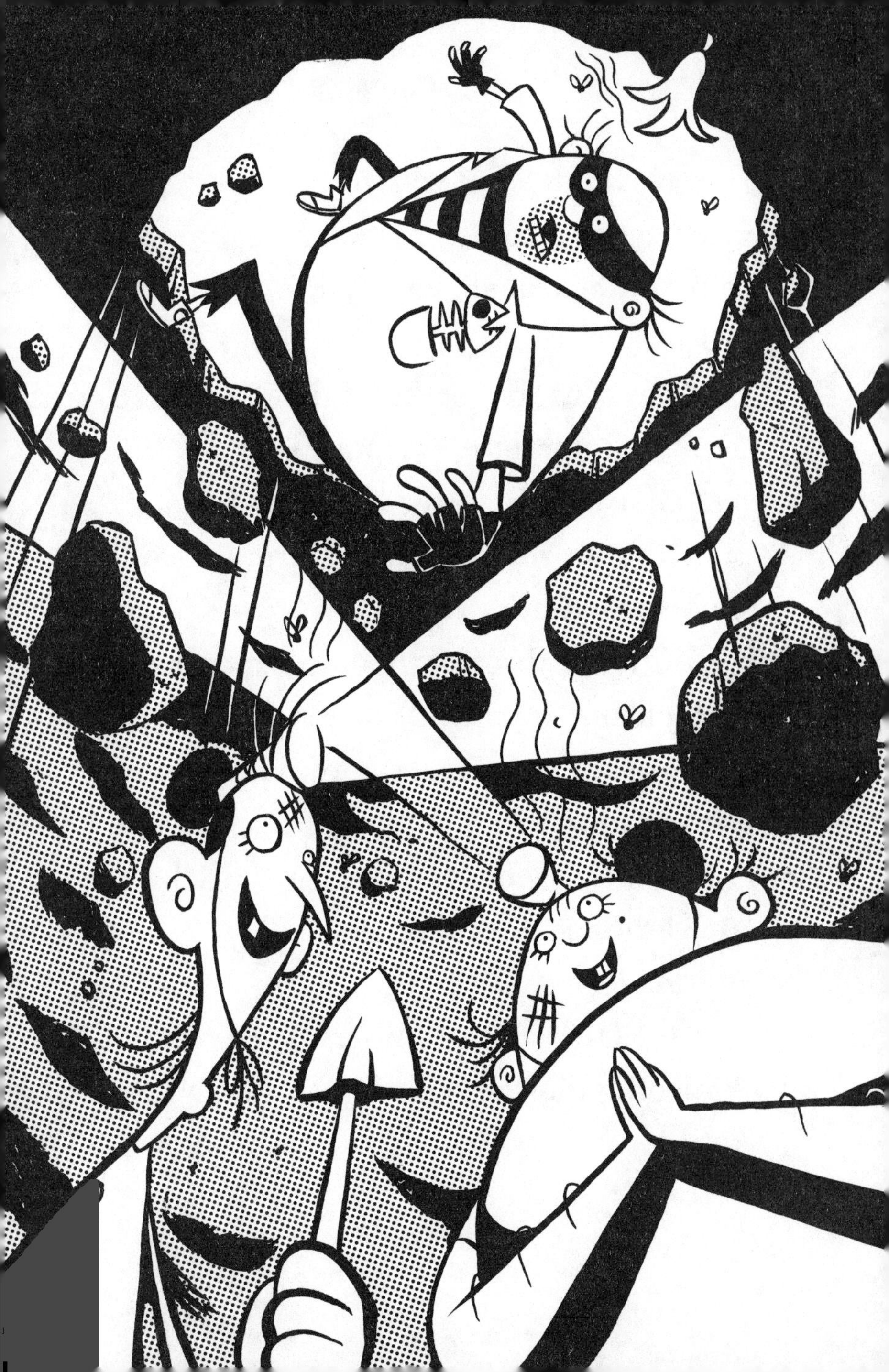

"We know what you mean," Puke said, giving her brother a hug. She handed him an extra shovel. "Now to rescue Filthy."

"Hey, I'm the leader of this gang, and don't you forget it!" Grunge said.

"Okay," Puke agreed.

"Now to rescue Filthy," Grunge said. Puke rolled her eyes.

With the three of them working hard, it took no time at all to reach the east side of the prison where Filthy was locked up.

"I hate Beederman, yes, I do. I hate Beederman. How about—"

Crash!

"—YOU." Like brother, like brother. Finishing their sentences was a McNasty thing.

"I never thought I'd get out of there. What do you say, Grunge, want to rob a few banks? I have a hankering for loot." Not money—loot.

"First things first," said Grunge. "I have a hankering for revenge. I do believe Melvin Beederman is about to have a very bad day."

"Beeder–who?" asked Mudball.

"Melvin Beederman, that superhero and all-around good guy."

"Yes. Of course. Exactly."

"He outsmarted us last time," Grunge said with a nasty smile. "That will never happen again."

PARTNERS IN UNCRIME

Crash!

Splat!

Thud!

Kabonk!

Melvin Beederman was up and flying on the fifth try. Once in a long while he was able to get airborne in one try, but not often. And not on this day.

Melvin was kept busy all morning and most of the afternoon. After all, it was rule number one in the Superhero's Code—"Never say no to a cry for help." And there were plenty of cries for help.

"Holy workaholic!" said Melvin. "I'm busy."

Holy workaholic, indeed! He *was* busy. Eleven bad guys caught before lunch. Seventeen caught after lunch. . . .

"That's twenty-eight bad guys in all," Melvin Beederman said out loud.

And not all of them had on clean underwear! Melvin couldn't turn off his x-ray vision. Headmaster Spinner had told him it was just a matter of time, but for right now the whole world was an underwear fashion show. Everywhere Melvin looked—underwear, underwear, underwear.

At three o'clock he gave his bad-guy catching a rest and flew over to the library to help his assistant with her math.

"Why are you smiling?" Candace asked suspiciously.

"I like smiling," said Melvin.

"This smile is different."

"I like math."

"That's not it either."

Melvin thought for a moment. He did feel extra good today. Why was today

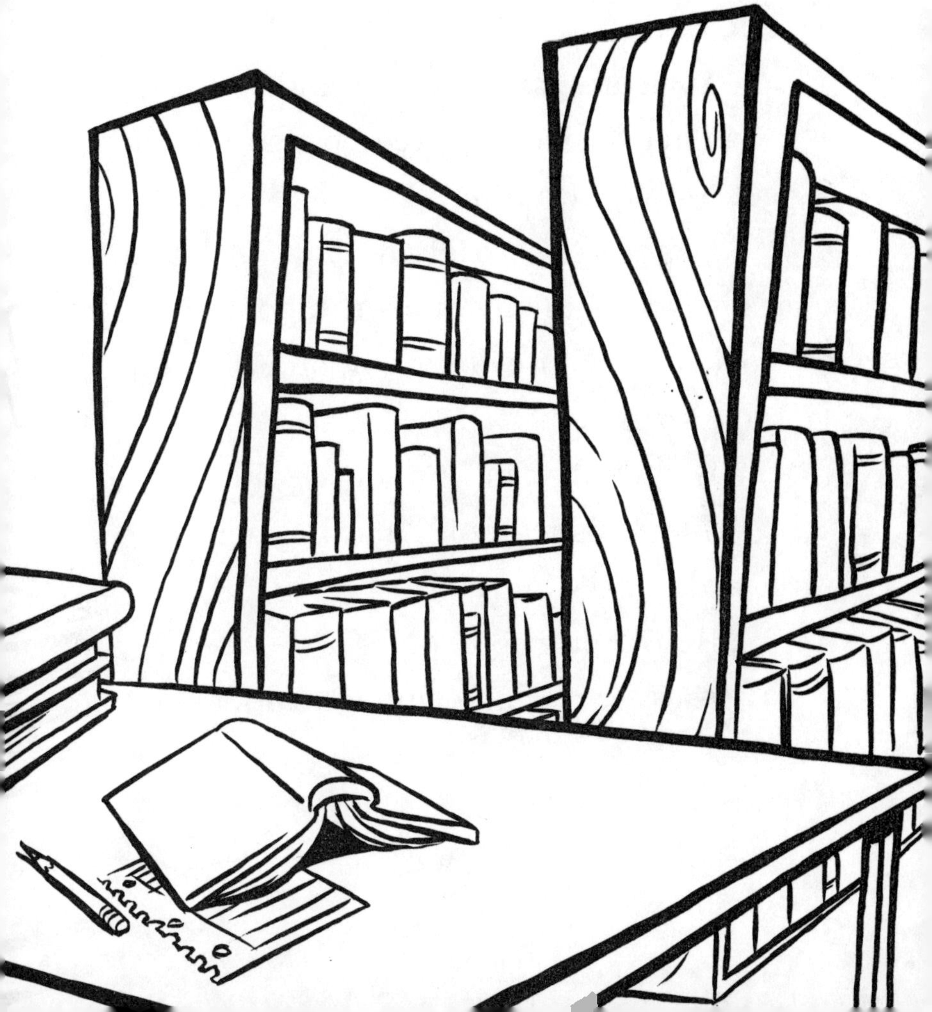

different from most days? Finally it came to him. "I have a roommate!" he said proudly. How could he have forgotten?

He told her the story of Hugo the rat—squeaks, pretzels, eyebrow wiggles, and all.

"You are so lucky," Candace said. "You get to live in a tree house *and* you get to live with a rat."

"I *am* lucky," Melvin said. "All you have is a room of your own, a pool in the backyard, your own puppy, and a family who loves you."

"Don't rub it in," Candace said.

They finished doing math. Then they heard it.

"Help! Somebody help!"

"A cry for help," Candace said.

"And what does the Superhero's Code say about that?" Melvin knew what the code said. He just wanted to test Candace. After all, he'd graduated from the Superhero Academy, and she hadn't. There were things she needed to know.

"Code, schmode. Let's go, Melvin. You're wasting time." Candace stuffed her books into her backpack and took off flying. "Up, up, and away."

Melvin got to his feet and looked at Candace hovering above the trees.

"Help! Somebody help!"

"Come on, Melvin," Candace said.

Melvin ran. "Up, up, and away." *Crash!*

"Up, up, and away." *Splat!*

Thud!

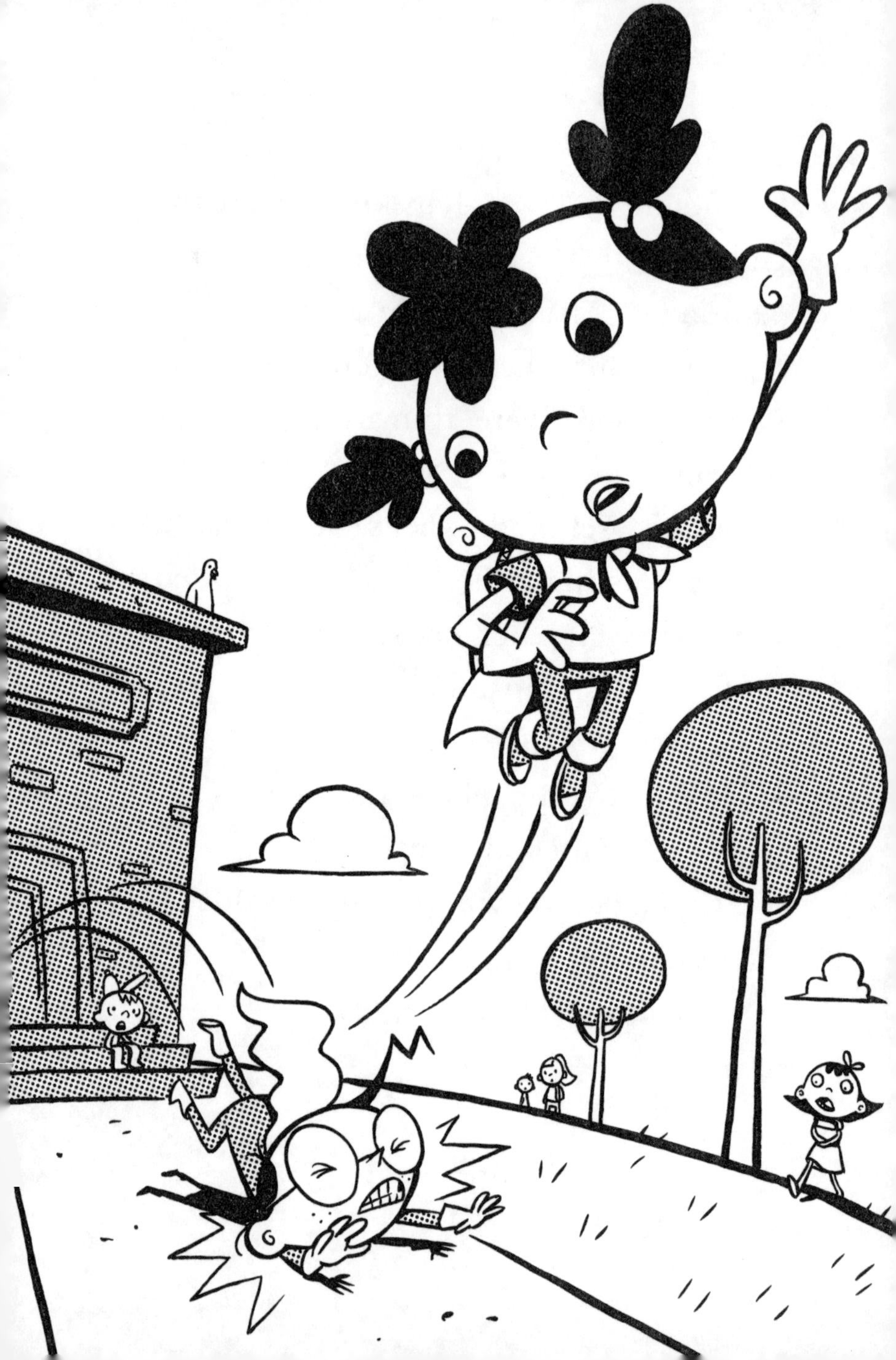

Kabonk!

Finally he joined Candace above the trees, and the two of them flew off together.

"You really need to work on your takeoffs, Melvin," Candace said. "People are beginning to talk."

"Don't rub it in," Melvin said.

THE FAMILY PLOT

Far below the county prison, the McNastys plotted their revenge. Or at least they tried to.

"We need an idea to get back at Melvin Beederman," Grunge McNasty said. "Let's put our heads together."

Mudball walked over and put her head next to Grunge's.

"I meant, let's think about it," Grunge said, blinking as the flashlight strapped to his sister's head shone in his eyes.

"Yes. Of course. Exactly," Mudball said.

"How do you get the best of a guy who can lift a school bus with one arm? Who can outrun a speeding bullet? Who can fly?" He looked at the dirty faces of his brother and two sisters. "Any ideas?"

"Well," Filthy McNasty began, "bologna almost worked last time."

"Almost isn't good enough," Grunge said. "You remember what happened. He ate the bologna and escaped."

Grunge paced around, thinking about it. Bologna was Melvin Beederman's weakness. He'd found that out from the unofficial Melvin Beederman Web site. And the bologna had worked—for a while. But then Melvin and his super-hero assistant ate the bologna, escaped, and sent Grunge and Filthy McNasty back to prison.

Melvin was just too smart. That was the thing. Grunge had heard that he was a math genius. And he'd even stunned his professors at the Superhero Academy with his oral report on the nature of good and evil.

Melvin Beederman had noggin power, a dangerous weapon for any superhero.

But what about his assistant? Grunge thought hard. Sure, Candace Brinkwater held the world record for the hundred-yard dash. Sure, she could slam-dunk and even fly. But was she as smart as Melvin Beederman?

Did she have noggin power?

Grunge smiled. And in the tunnel, where the only light was the glow from the flashlights strapped to the heads of his sisters, that smile looked pretty creepy. Pretty creepy indeed.

"Ladies and gentleman," Grunge said, "I think I have a plan."

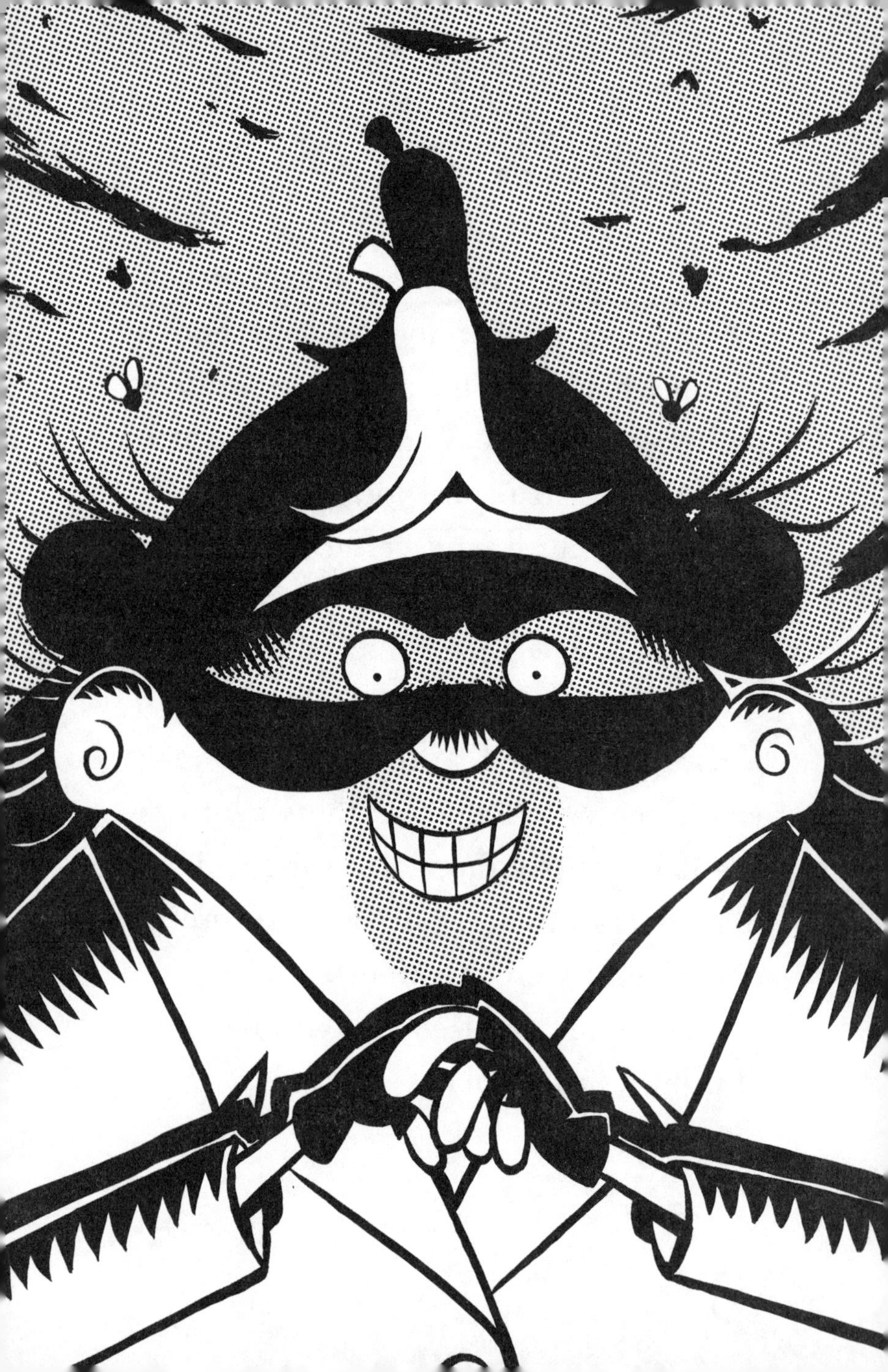

Grunge, Filthy, and Puke McNasty began walking away, but Mudball McNasty stayed in the tunnel. She searched high and low. There was not a lady or gentleman anywhere.

"I meant you guys," Grunge called back to her.

"Yes. Of course. Exactly," Mudball said as she ran to catch up.

CANDACE CRACKS THE CODE . . . SORT OF

Melvin Beederman and Candace Brinkwater were too busy to think about the McNasty Brothers. Or the McNasty Sisters, for that matter. The superheroes had more important things to worry about.

Right now there was a cry for help, and the code was pretty clear on that subject. Problem was, only Melvin had graduated from the Superhero Academy. Candace had not. So only Melvin knew the code. And the code was clear, not only about never saying no to a cry for help, but also about showing up just in the nick of time. The code also explained what you should say once you got there. Superhero lingo. There was a right way and a wrong way.

Melvin thought about this as they flew over the city. Candace didn't know the code. And she didn't seem to care.

The superheroes zoomed between the tall buildings of downtown Los Angeles. Since they were in a hurry, Melvin paused only once to flex and admire his muscles in the mirrored glass. He saw his reflection in 57 different windows on the building in front of him, and in 39 windows in the building behind him.

"That's 96 windows," he said quickly.

Ah . . . math.

"Help. Somebody help!"

The cry for help snapped Melvin out of his flexing. And his math problem.

Below him he saw a boy standing on a crowded sidewalk. Candace dropped to the pavement while Melvin stayed hovering overhead. He was up and flying and didn't want to have to start over.

The boy looked at Candace in front of him and at Melvin above. Then he pointed down the street.

"Skateboard stealer."

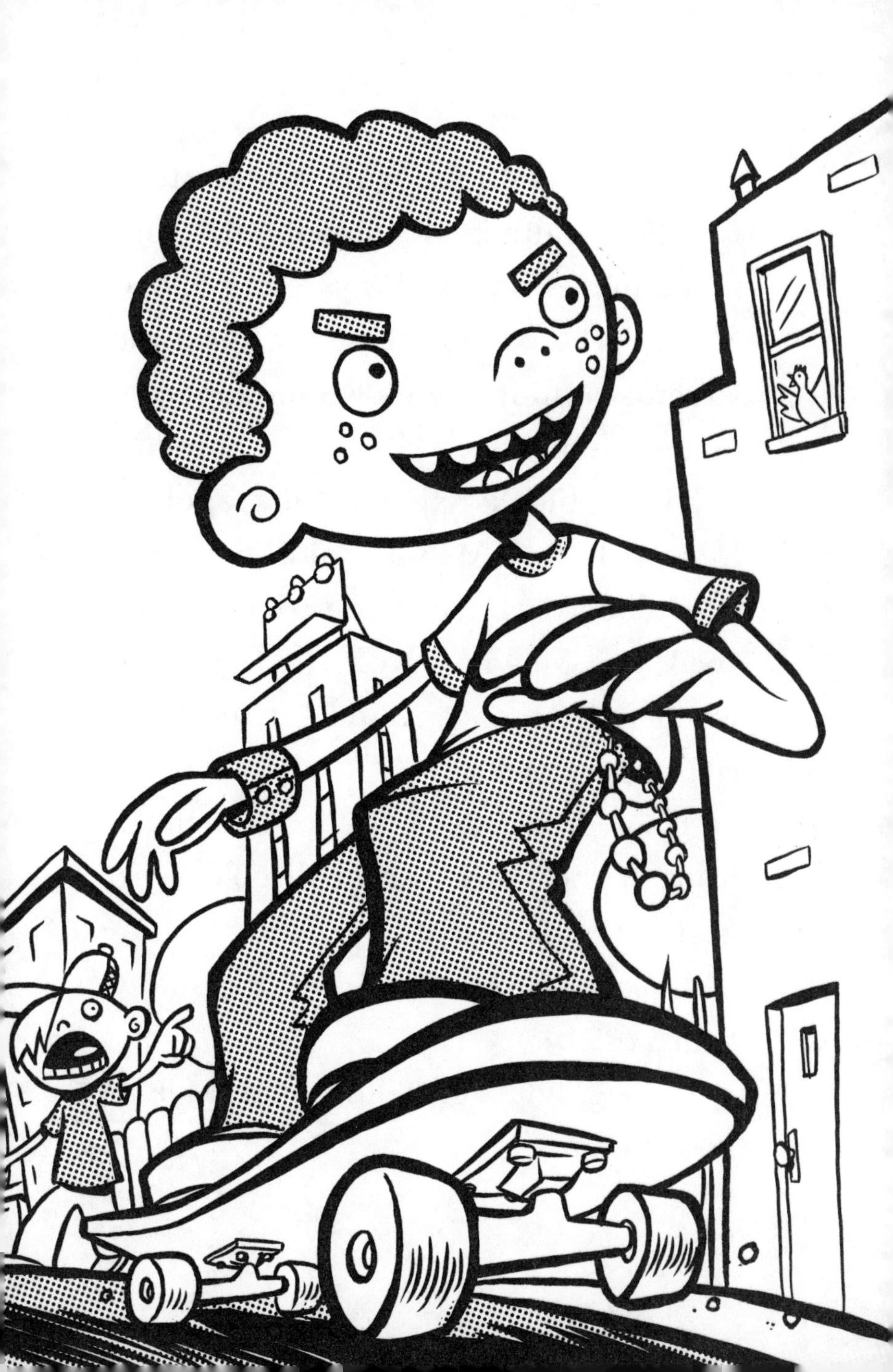

Without waiting for the whole story, Candace launched herself—up and flying in one try, as always—and joined Melvin. The two of them flew down the street, scanning the crowd for someone on a skateboard.

Three blocks ahead they spotted him. "There," Melvin said, pointing. "Skateboarder, red underwear." They sped up. Melvin hardly had time to wonder if Candace would get the lingo right this time.

They dropped to the pavement in front of the skateboarder. "Don't be so hasty," Candace said.

"I beg your pardon?" said the skateboard thief.

"I beg your pardon?" said Melvin Beederman.

"I mean, uh, come out with your hands up," Candace said.

"Is this some kind of joke?"

"Stop in the name of the law."

The skateboard thief didn't stick around for Candace to come up with the right lingo. He took off again. "Superheroes," he muttered.

"I order you to halt!" Candace yelled after him. She looked at Melvin. "How about a little help, partner in uncrime?"

"Not so fast," Melvin said.

"That's it!" Candace turned back to the skateboarder. "Not so—"

The skateboarder was gone, of course. And with the street so crowded, Melvin didn't feel like trying to fly again. Besides, on a good day he could run as fast as a speeding bullet. Candace

Brinkwater launched herself, while Melvin stayed on the ground.

"You do the talking when we catch him," Candace said.

"I will," Melvin said.

It was a busy afternoon, all things considered. Candace messed up a few more times in the lingo department. Once when a woman thanked them for saving her child who had wandered out onto a busy highway, Candace replied, "No prob, lady."

The proper response according to the code was "Just doing our job, ma'am."

Candace was clueless about the code. But she sure could fly!

By the end of the day the partners had captured two skateboard stealers, one bank robber, and a couple of car thieves, plus a streaker and one guy with very bad language.

And they saw lots and lots of underwear—in every color and in every style. Some people just weren't meant to be seen in their underwear. In fact, most people weren't meant to be seen in their underwear.

"Gotta be home by dinner," Candace reminded Melvin.

"Right. Let's go. Up, up, and away."

Crash!

Splat!

Thud!

Kabonk!

"Some things never change," Melvin said, as he finally became airborne on the fifth try.

"You're telling me," Candace said.

SIX BULLIES
AND A SUPERHERO

Candace Brinkwater liked school these days. Especially recess. In the past she had hated recess because she was so lousy at games. You name it and she was terrible at it. Kickball—horrible. Tetherball—a joke. And the other kids just laughed whenever she stepped onto the basketball courts.

That was before she became a superhero, of course. Now she was the first one picked in every team sport.

"We get Candace on our team."

"No, we do."

And so she liked school. She liked recess. She liked being liked.

Problem was, not everybody liked her. And Candace was enjoying school way too much to notice. While she was kicking kickballs over the school fence and scoring hundreds of points on the basketball courts, the school bullies were putting their heads together.

Johnny Fink and Knucklehead Wilson were the main school bullies, but they weren't the only ones. There was also Frank, Joe, Jimmy . . . and a kid named Fred.

Johnny was the leader of this newly banded-together group of bullies. In the past these boys had been enemies. But now they were pals. They had joined forces against their common enemy: Candace Brinkwater. World-record holder in the hundred-yard dash, the only person ever to score 500 points in a basketball game . . . the only third-grader who could fly.

They had a plan to get Candace Brinkwater and return to the life they knew best: picking on people.

"Now, do we all know what we're going to do?" Johnny asked. They had met under the goalposts on the soccer field to discuss the matter.

"Yes," all of them said, one after the other. "Tomorrow at recess Candace gets it."

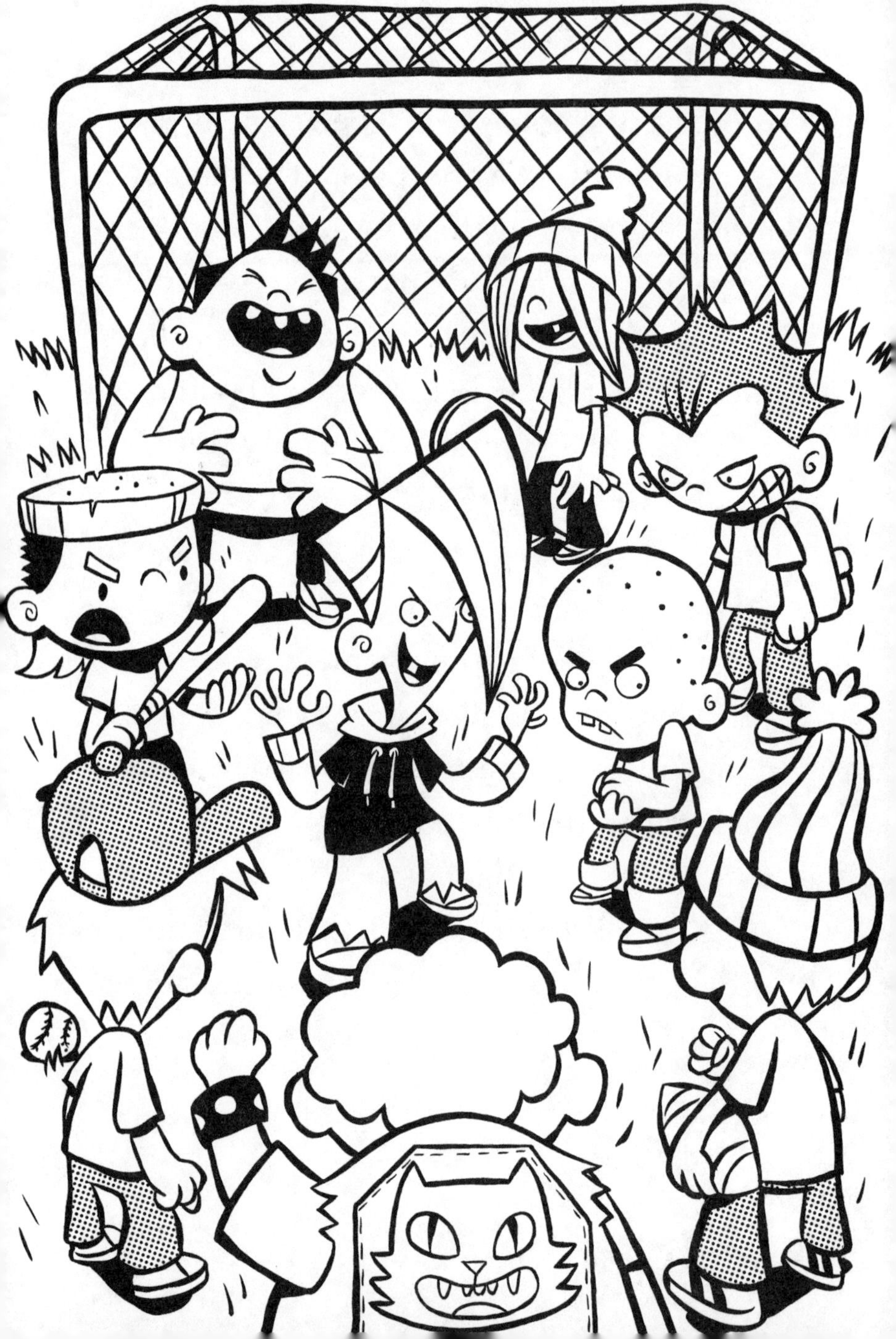

"Okay, let's all synchronize our watches," Johnny said.

"We're not wearing watches."

"I know, but I've always wanted to say that."

HOLY COUCH POTATOES!

Melvin Beederman flew back to his tree house after seeing Candace Brinkwater home. It wasn't part of the Superhero's Code to always be a gentleman, but he knew it must be an unwritten rule somewhere. And certainly it made sense.

It had been many hours since he'd left. Would the rat he had shared pretzels and watched cartoons with still be there? He thought of Hugo as his pet.

But what did Hugo think? Was Melvin Beederman someone he wanted to spend time with, or was he just a funny-looking guy in a cape who happened to be stocked with tasty food?

As Melvin stepped through the door, his biggest question was: Did he have a roommate or did he not?

The rat was there waiting. "Squeak?" he said to Melvin with a twitch of his long rat whiskers.

Melvin took this to mean, "Break out the pretzels, mister, and let's see what's on TV."

Melvin did just that. He broke out the pretzels and the root beer and snapped on the television. "Squeak squeak," he said to the rat, giving his eyebrows a wiggle. He thought he'd just said, "Another episode of *The Adventures of Thunderman*?" or possibly, "Do you have a girlfriend?" He wasn't sure.

They found a rerun of *The Adventures of Thunderman* and settled in, eating pretzels and sipping root beer.

They sat and sat.

Outside it was quiet. Way too quiet, Melvin thought.

"Holy couch potatoes!" he cried, jumping to his feet. "If I didn't know better, I'd say trouble was brewing."

THE BAD GUYS' LAIR

Holy couch potatoes, indeed! Trouble *was* brewing.

All the way on the other side of town, the McNastys were in their lair. Not hideout—lair. Only good guys and minor bad guys had hideouts. Major bad guys had lairs. It was where they devised sinister plots and cooked up devious ideas.

"You're looking rather sinister," Filthy McNasty said to his brother.

"Oh, really?" Grunge said. "I was going for devious."

"That too. What devious ideas are you coming up with?"

"Tell you in a second." Grunge turned and yelled into the kitchen, "Where's that tea?" Mudball and Puke McNasty were busy rustling up some tasty vittles. Not food—vittles. Grunge McNasty didn't particularly like tea. He just believed in brewing more than one thing at a time.

This was not part of the bad guy's code, but it was very common.

The McNasty Sisters brought the vittles and tea into the living area of the lair. Grunge McNasty took a sip of tea. "How do I look?" he asked Mudball and Puke.

"Sinister," Mudball said.

"I'd say devious," Puke said.

"Good. Either one of those will work. Now, tell me, what is Melvin Beederman's weakness?"

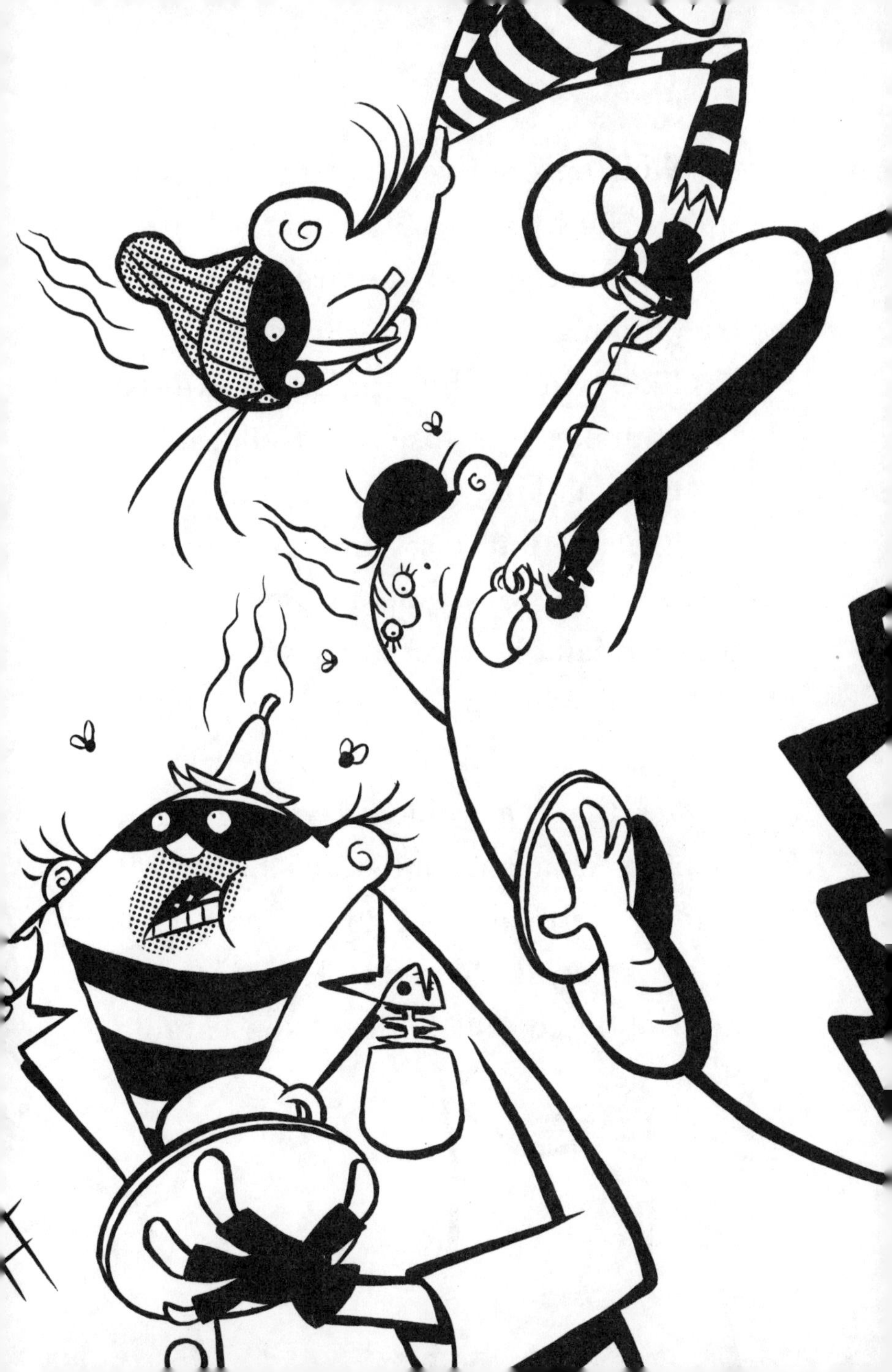

"Well, he's not very good at stopping trains," Filthy said.

"He can't get off the ground in one try," Puke said.

"No, I mean his major weakness. What makes him lose his strength?"

"Bologna," they all said in unison.

"Exactly. But last time he ate the bologna and was able to escape. This time we can't let that happen."

"I've never heard of non-eatable bologna," Filthy said.

"Yes, that is a problem." Grunge began to pace, chanting under his breath, "I hate Beederman, yes I do . . ."

He stopped. "Non-eatable bologna," he wondered out loud. "Non-eatable bologna . . ."

The McNastys sipped their tea and ate their vittles. They stayed up all night long discussing the problem. In the end they decided that the key to Melvin Beederman was his assistant, Candace Brinkwater. If they got her, they'd get him.

When morning came, Grunge, Filthy, Puke, and Mudball all had the same look in their eye. Sinister. Or maybe it was devious.

Trouble was no longer brewing. It was *brewed*.

DOG PILE ON BRINKWATER!

It was a normal day for Candace Brinkwater. She skipped the bus and flew to school. The bullies behaved themselves. She slam-dunked basketballs. She punted kickballs over fences. She got a C– in math.

A normal day.

And pretty darn quiet.

She might have thought it was *too* quiet if she had been paying attention.

But Candace wasn't. She was distracted by all the slam-dunking and kickball kicking.

So she didn't see it coming when she walked into the girls' bathroom during lunch.

Suddenly the doors to the stalls flew open, and there stood Johnny Fink, along with Knucklehead Wilson and the other school bullies—Frank, Joe, Jimmy . . . a kid named Fred.

"Get her!" Johnny yelled.

Before Candace could think to move, the boys pounced.

"Holy dog pile," Candace said from the bottom of the stack.

Holy dog pile, indeed! She had no less than six boys on top of her. Candace was confused. Was this some sort of group hug? These were the school bullies. They were supposed to *hate* good guys.

"Okay, get her cape," Johnny said.

Candace realized this was no group hug. It was time to get busy.

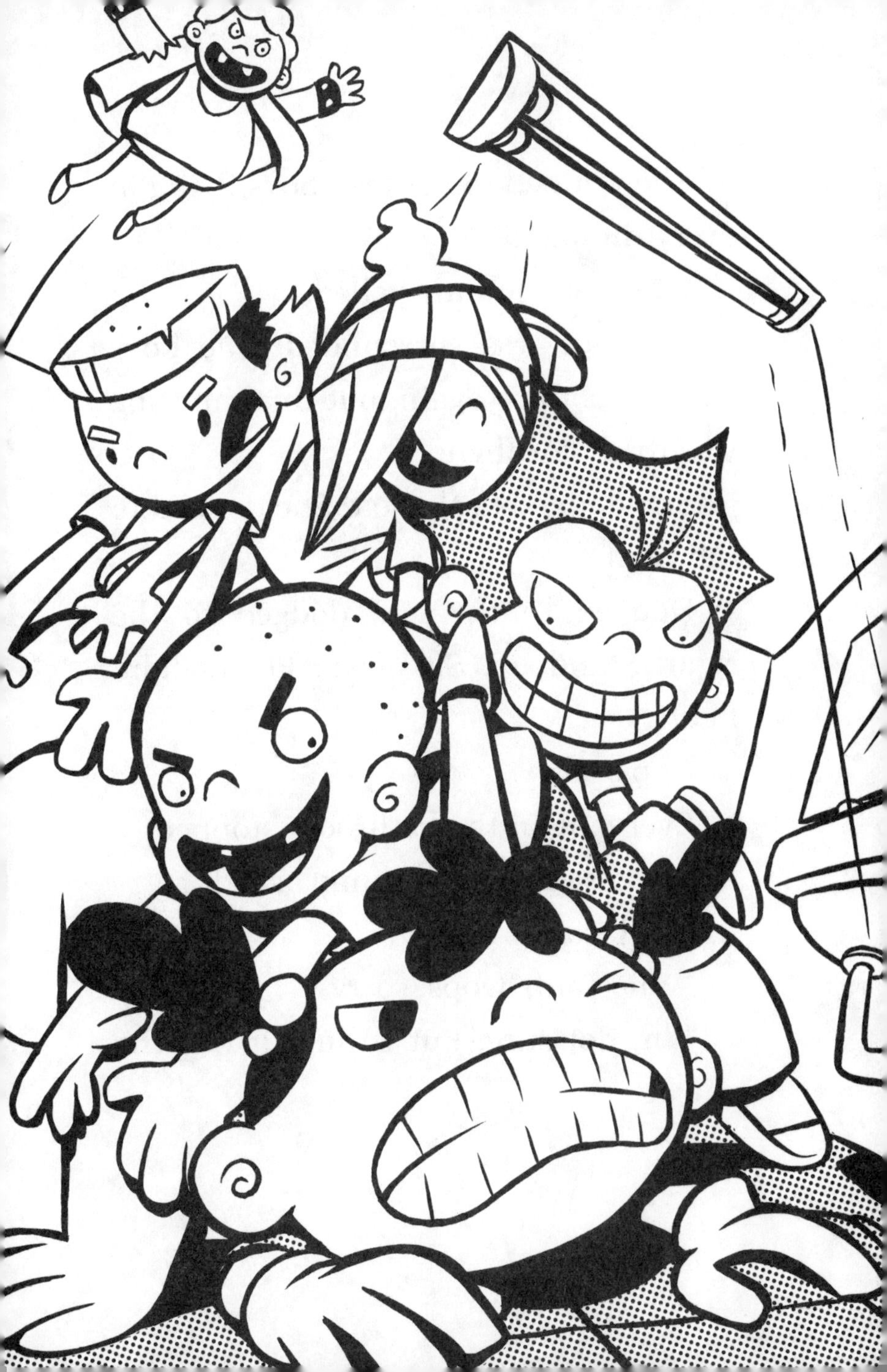

She jumped to her feet, boys flying in every direction.

"Get her!" Johnny yelled.

Candace was surrounded. The boys tried to pounce again, but this time she was ready for them.

She dodged to the left. She dodged to the right.

Dodged to the left, dodged to the right. Stand up. Sit down. Fight, fight, fight!

Oops, sorry.

Everyone in the bathroom stopped.

"Who said that?" Johnny asked.

"Who said what?"

"Who said, 'Oops, sorry'?"

"I'm not sure. But I think it was the narrator."

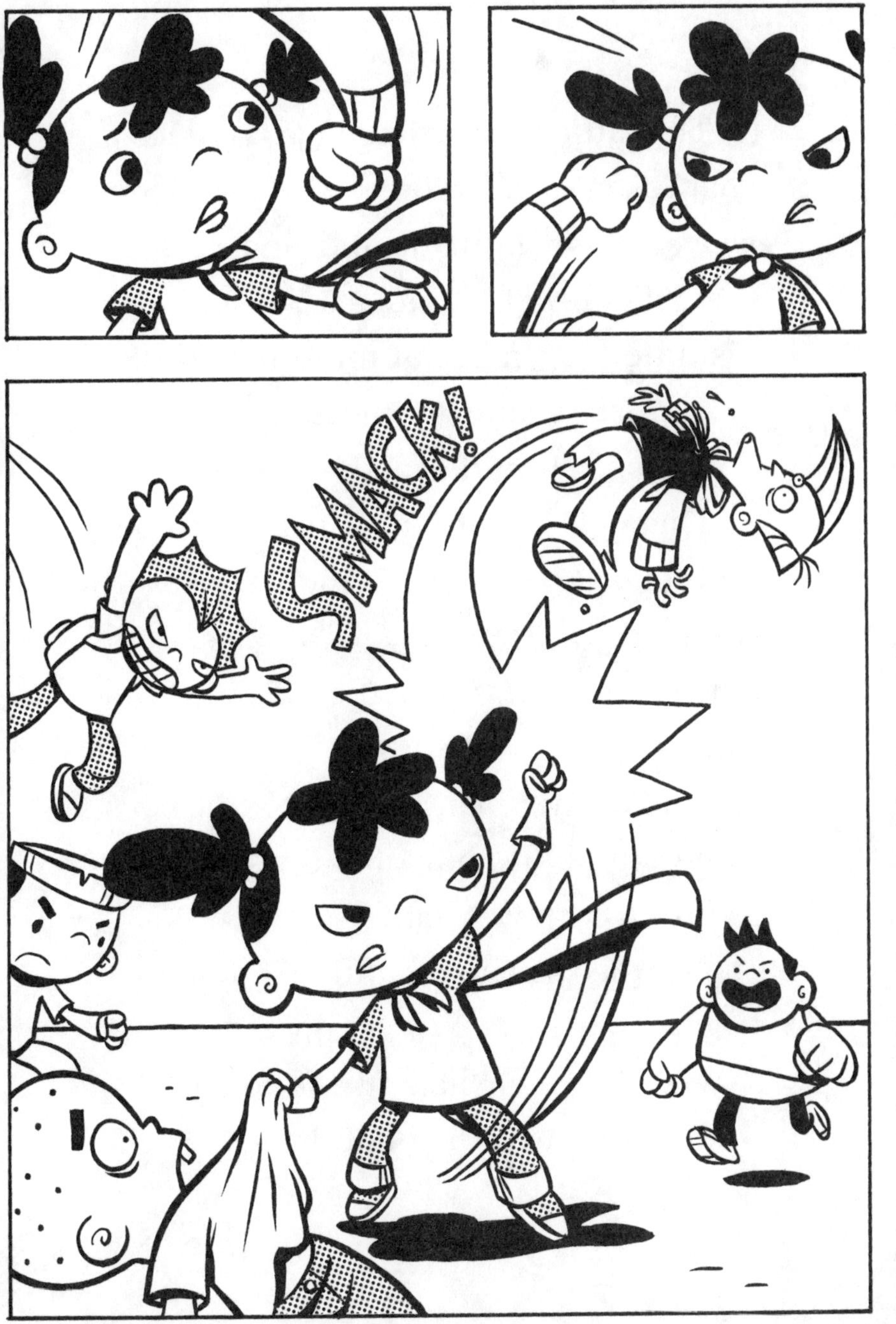
SMACK!

This little distraction gave Candace a chance to sneak around the boys. She shoved them from behind and each of them flew headfirst into a toilet stall. Not just into the stalls, but into the toilets!

Candace's aim was perfect.

"My aim is perfect," she said.

Then she raced out of the bathroom and found a teacher. "Some boys are in the girls' bathroom," Candace told her. "They're washing their hair in the toilets."

Sure enough, a moment later the boys came stumbling out of the girls' bathroom, all with wet hair.

"To the principal's office, boys," the teacher said.

Washing their hair in the toilets . . . some things were just not done.

THINGS GET SINISTER

Later that day, a voice came over the intercom in Candace's class. "Please send Candace Brinkwater to the office immediately."

Candace put down her pencil and stood up. She was doing a difficult math problem and was glad to have a break. She walked down the hall, thinking how great life was. She had never flushed six boys before, and she was feeling pretty good about it.

"Six of them," she said to herself proudly. "Six against one. You're *bad*, Candace Brinkwater."

Had she known the Superhero's Code, of course, she would have known better than to let her victories go to her head. A superhero always had to be on the alert. And Candace was too busy high-fiving herself at the moment to pay attention.

Big mistake.

Something sinister could sneak right up and bite her on the . . . uh . . . toe.

Candace got to the school office, but the secretary wasn't there. The place was empty. There was also a strange smell in the air.

"Holy gas mask!" Candace said as her eyes began to water. "That's nasty!"

Holy gas mask, indeed! It was nasty.

"Hello?" Candace said, pinching her nose.

No answer.

"Knock knock. Anyone home?"

Silence.

Candace walked into the principal's office and there she saw it. Bologna. An extra-long bologna submarine sandwich, to be exact. The principal and the school secretary were lying on the floor, tied up and gagged.

Candace felt the strength drain from her body. She dropped to her knees, gasping, "Can't . . . move . . . get . . . me . . . out . . . of . . . here."

"Glad to oblige," said a voice from behind her.

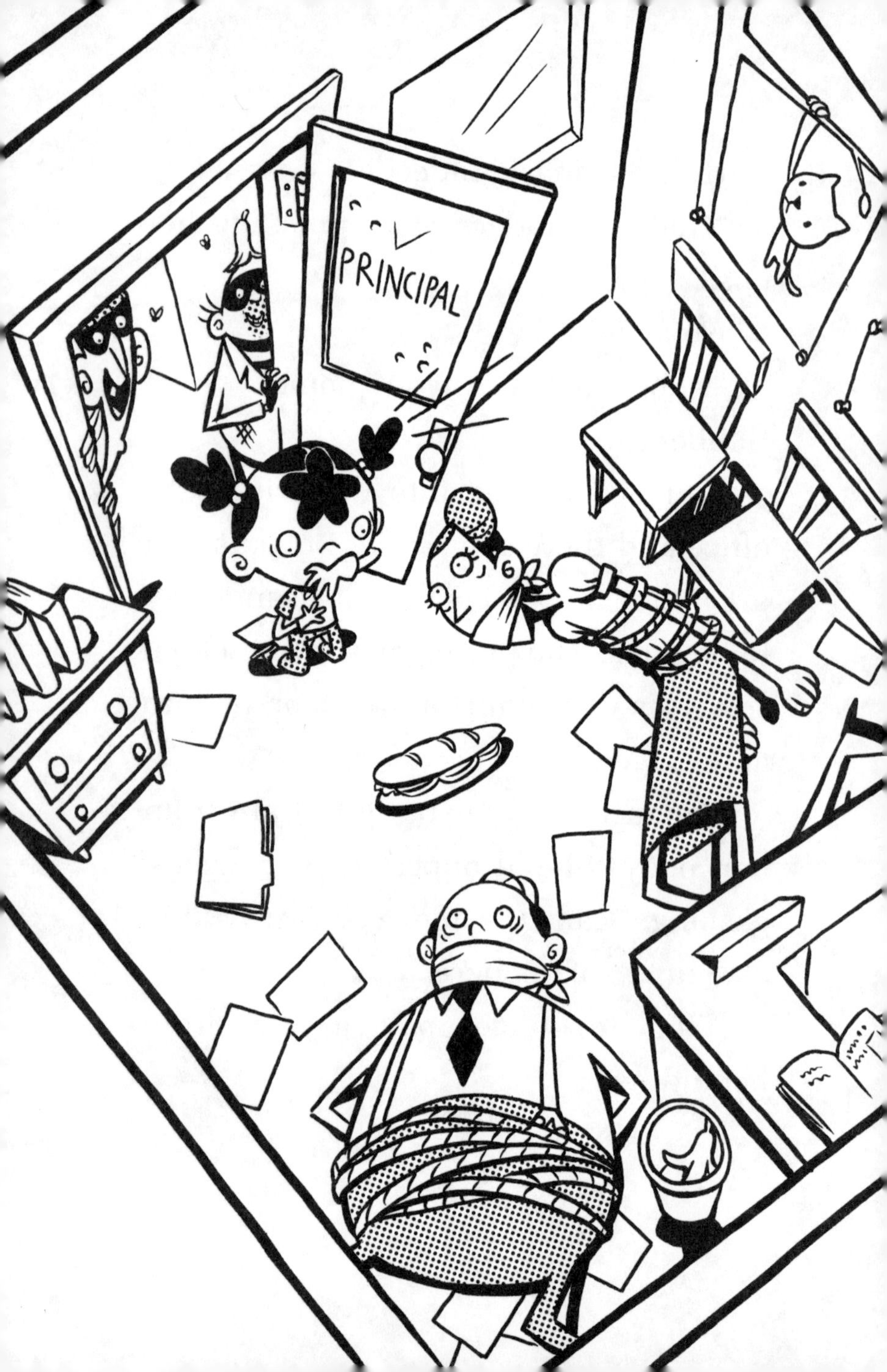
PRINCIPAL

Candace turned to see Filthy and Grunge McNasty. So *that's* what smelled so bad.

"Grab the bologna, Filthy," Grunge said. "I'll grab the girl."

Grunge picked up Candace and threw her over his shoulder. With the bologna sandwich so close by, she was too weak to resist.

A minivan was idling in the school parking lot. *Now, there's one sinister-looking minivan,* thought Candace as Grunge McNasty stuffed her inside.

"Where are you taking me?" she gasped.

"Where else? Our lair."

"Don't you mean hideout?"

"I mean lair. No minor bad guys in this story."

That was funny. Candace seemed to remember flushing a few minor bad guys earlier in the day.

As the minivan sped through the city, she thought about all that had happened. How could a day that had started out so good turn out to be so rotten?

MEANWHILE . . .

While Candace Brinkwater was busy flushing heads and getting kidnapped, Melvin Beederman was busy trying to launch himself.

Crash!

Splat!

Thud!

Kabonk!

He'd heard a cry for help while watching *The Adventures of Thunderman* and had to leave right in the middle of the good part. Did Thunderman and his assistant, Thunder Thighs, get the bad guys in the end? Melvin wasn't able to stick around to find out. After all, the code was the code. But he hoped Hugo, his pet rat and roommate, would fill him in on the details when he got home.

"Squeak squeak," he had told him before he left. He thought this meant "Take good notes and fill me in when I get home." But it might have meant, "Would you care for a slice of pie?" He was never really sure. Rat talk wasn't exactly the same as gerbilspeak.

But now Melvin was up and flying, searching for the voice he had heard earlier.

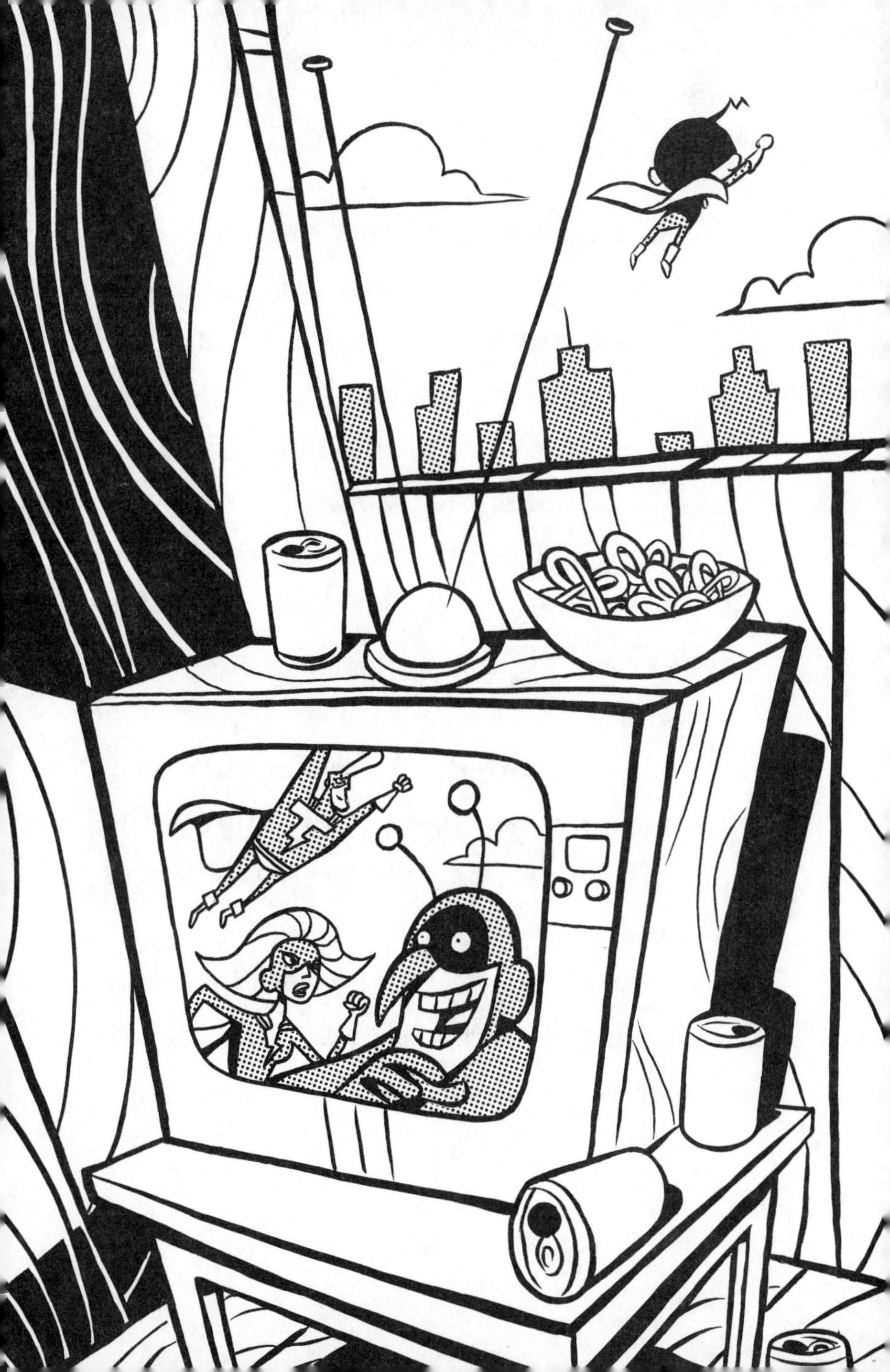

"Help!" came the voice again.

Melvin zoomed between the tall buildings of downtown Los Angeles. Below him he saw 28 red SUVs and 63 white SUVs (minivans were a thing of the past in this town). "That's 91 SUVs in all," he said quickly.

If only Hugo was good at math, Melvin thought, home life would be perfect.

"Help!"

Melvin spotted a lady standing on a busy sidewalk. She pointed down the street. "There was a purse snatcher. He's getting away."

With his extra-keen eyesight, Melvin spotted the thief. He also spotted his underwear . . . which was spotted!

"Be right back," he called to the lady, then zoomed ahead and dropped in front of the purse snatcher. "Not so fast!"

Melvin returned the purse to its owner.

"How can I ever thank you?" asked the lady, checking to see that her money was still there.

"Just doing my job, ma'am."

Ah . . . the code. Melvin knew the code like the back of his kneecap.

He bowed. "Have a nice d—"

And that's when he heard it.

"Can't . . . move . . . get . . . me . . . out . . . of . . . here."

Candace Brinkwater, his partner in uncrime, was in trouble!

Melvin knew he had to save the day.

"Excuse me, ma'am, but I have to save the day." Melvin tried to launch himself right there in broad daylight, right in front of everyone. And . . .

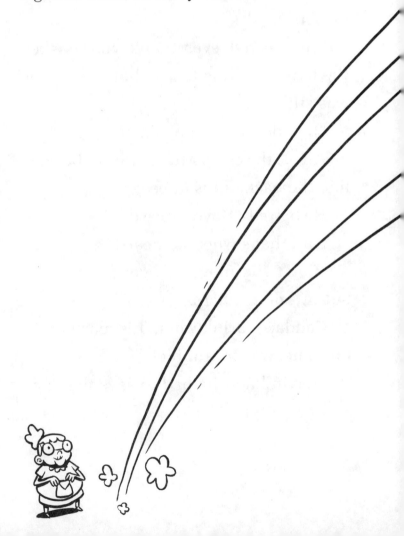

He was up and flying on the first try! But he didn't have time to pat himself on the back.

What have you gotten yourself into, Candace? he thought to himself as he zoomed to the rescue.

THOSE DEVIOUS McNASTYS

It just so happened that the workers at the Acme Bologna Company were on strike. They were picketing in front of the Acme headquarters, where the slogan was *Acme Bologna, We're Not Too Shabby*.

Not too shabby, indeed! Acme Bologna was terrific. And there was a lot of it. The company just treated its workers terribly.

Hence the strike.

This worked to the McNastys' advantage. While the workers were striking in front of the building, no one was paying attention to the back entrance. So no one saw a sinister-looking minivan pull up. No one saw two sinister-looking men and two sinister-looking women get out, carrying a young girl in a cape.

"I love being devious," Grunge McNasty said, kicking in the back door.

"What a coincidence," said his brother, Filthy. "I love being sinister."

"We must be related."

They entered the big warehouse, where there was six thousand pounds of bologna.

"Wow!" said Grunge. "That looks like

six thousand pounds of bologna. What do you have to say about that, Miss Brinkwater?"

"What do I have to say?" Candace said weakly.

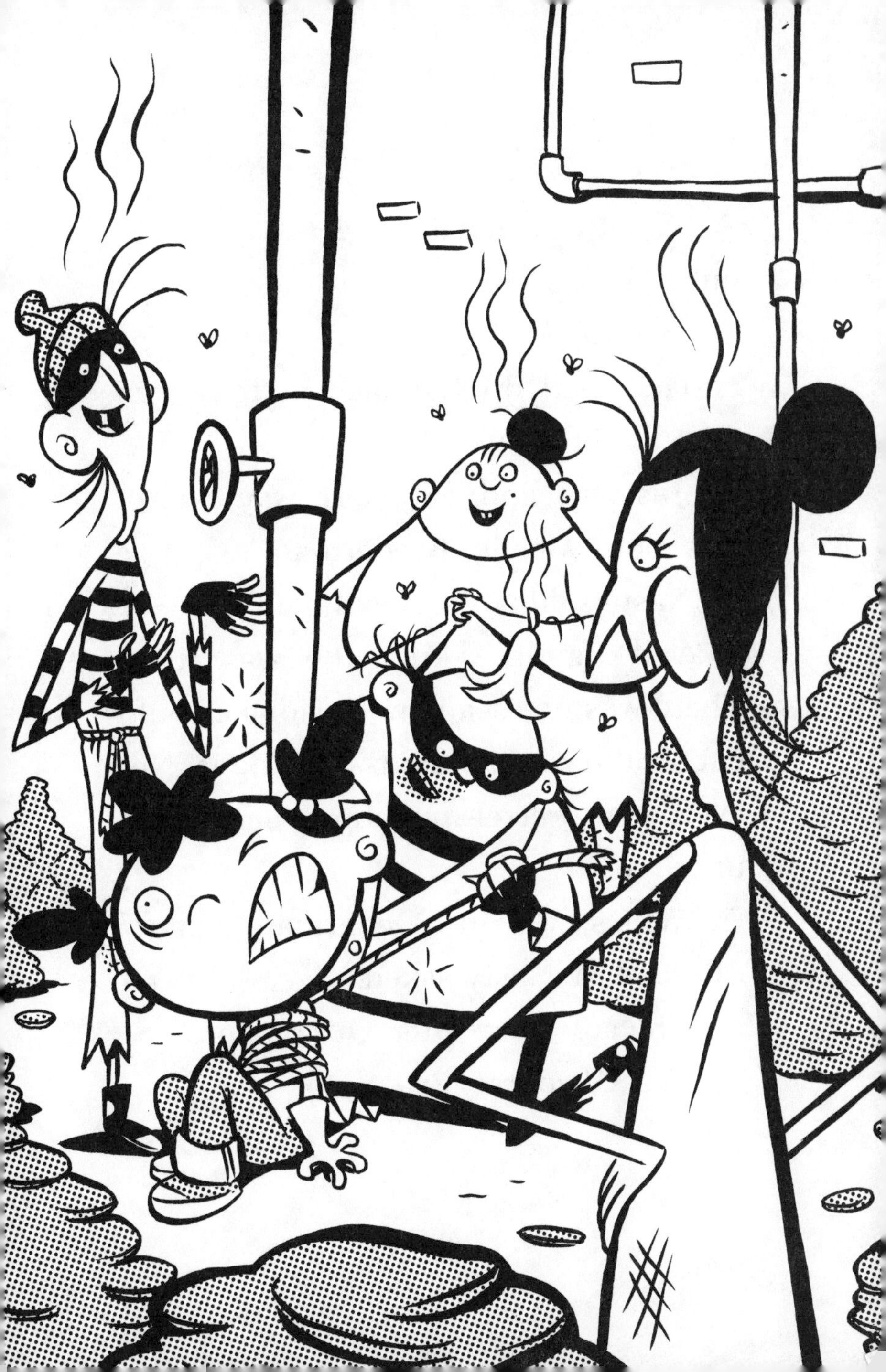

"Yes."

"Can't . . . move . . . get . . . me . . . out . . . of . . . here."

"No way."

They tied up Candace in the room with the bologna.

"Just try and eat your way out of this one, Melvin Beederman," Grunge McNasty said with an evil laugh.

And Candace knew he was right. There was no escape now. No one could eat six thousand pounds of bologna. Not even her pretzel-munching partner in uncrime.

"Who's Melvin Beederman again?" Mudball McNasty asked.

"The guy we're after. Our enemy."

"Yes. Of course. Exactly."

BEEDERMAN TO THE RESCUE

Melvin Beederman zoomed. He was an expert zoomer. Once he got off the ground he could zoom like nobody's business.

Once he got off the ground.

And now, with Candace Brinkwater in trouble, there was no time to hover and flex at his reflection in the mirrored glass. But that didn't stop Melvin from thinking about it as he flew between the tall buildings of the city. *I'll do it later,* he told himself. And he made a mental note to do just that.

It was a rotten shame to see his reflection and not get to flex.

Melvin flew and listened for Candace's cry for help. Then he heard it.

"Can't . . . move . . . get . . . me . . . out . . . of . . . here."

Candace was growing weaker by the minute, the six thousand pounds of bologna taking every last bit of strength she had.

Melvin knew she was growing weaker. He also knew why. Bologna!

And from the sound of her voice, it had to be a lot of bologna. Not just a sandwich full—something more.

"Holy overeating! That's got to be a ton of bologna," he said.

Holy overeating, indeed! It was three tons to be exact.

But where was Candace?

He zigzagged between the tall buildings. He shot out toward the beach and over the hills into the Valley. He listened. But there were no more cries for help.

Then he smelled it. Something awful, something horrible, something . . . nasty. If he didn't know better, he'd say the McNastys were on the loose again.

Melvin sped up and followed his nose. The smell got worse. And worse. His eyes began to water.

Below him he spotted some people walking back and forth in front of a building, carrying signs—DOWN WITH ACME BOLOGNA and BOYCOTT ACME BOLOGNA and ACME BOLOGNA STINKS!

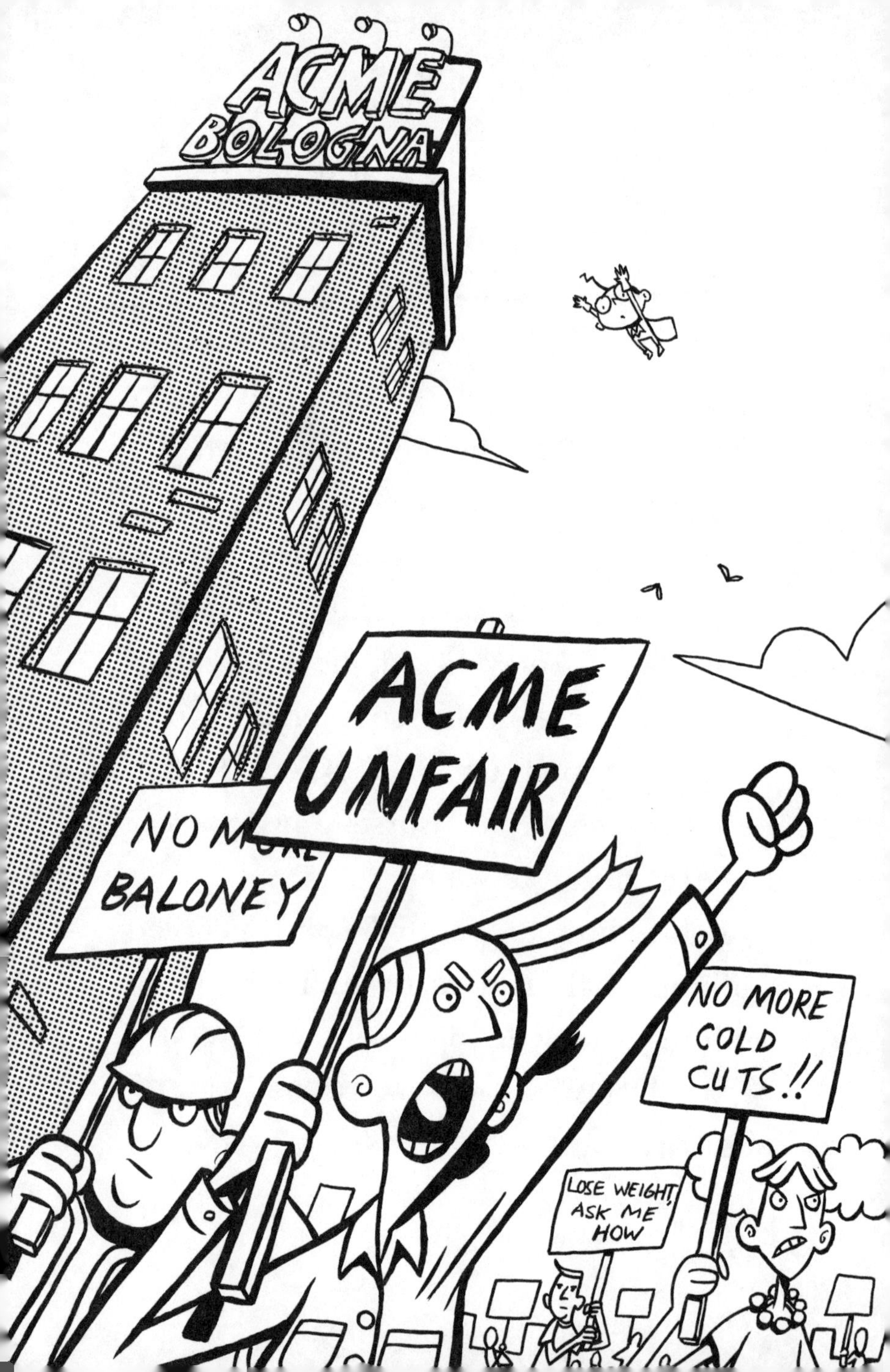
ACME BOLOGNA
ACME UNFAIR
NO MORE BALONEY
NO MORE COLD CUTS!!
LOSE WEIGHT, ASK ME HOW

Melvin sniffed. *Well, something stinks,* he thought. But he was pretty sure it wasn't bologna. Now, as he hovered over the Acme Bologna Company head-quarters, he could do nothing but trust his nose.

Something nasty was afoot. And that nasty something had to be the brothers themselves. The McNasty Brothers, those notorious bank robbers and all-around bad guys.

Melvin didn't know about the McNasty Sisters or about the prison break. He only knew what his nose was telling him. And he trusted it.

After all, nose power was second only to noggin power.

Then, very faintly, he heard it again.

"Can't . . . move . . . get . . . me . . . out . . . of . . . here."

"Well, bless my nose!" Melvin said out loud. "You're the best nose a guy ever had."

Candace Brinkwater was inside the building. Melvin knew that. He also knew it had to be the McNasty Brothers behind it all.

It was way too crowded in front of the building, so Melvin zipped around to the back entrance. He was going to kick in the door, but discovered it had already been done, which of course took some of the fun out of the rescue. Though it wasn't part of the code, super-heroes often kicked in doors, and they hardly ever repaired the damage when they were finished.

Melvin put this thought aside. He'd find another door to kick in later. Right now Candace Brinkwater, his partner in uncrime, needed him.

He swung open the door that had already been kicked in. Instantly his head began to swim. His legs went wobbly and he dropped to his knees. "Can't . . . move . . . get . . . me . . . out . . . of . . . here," he gasped.

SIX THOUSAND POUNDS
OF BOLOGNA

Melvin Beederman was defenseless against the McNasty Brothers. But who were these others with them? They smelled as bad. They looked as ugly. They had either a sinister or a devious look on their faces. Were they related?

Grunge McNasty spoke up in answer to Melvin's unspoken question. "These are my sisters, Mudball and Puke McNasty. Perhaps you have heard of them—notorious jewel thieves and

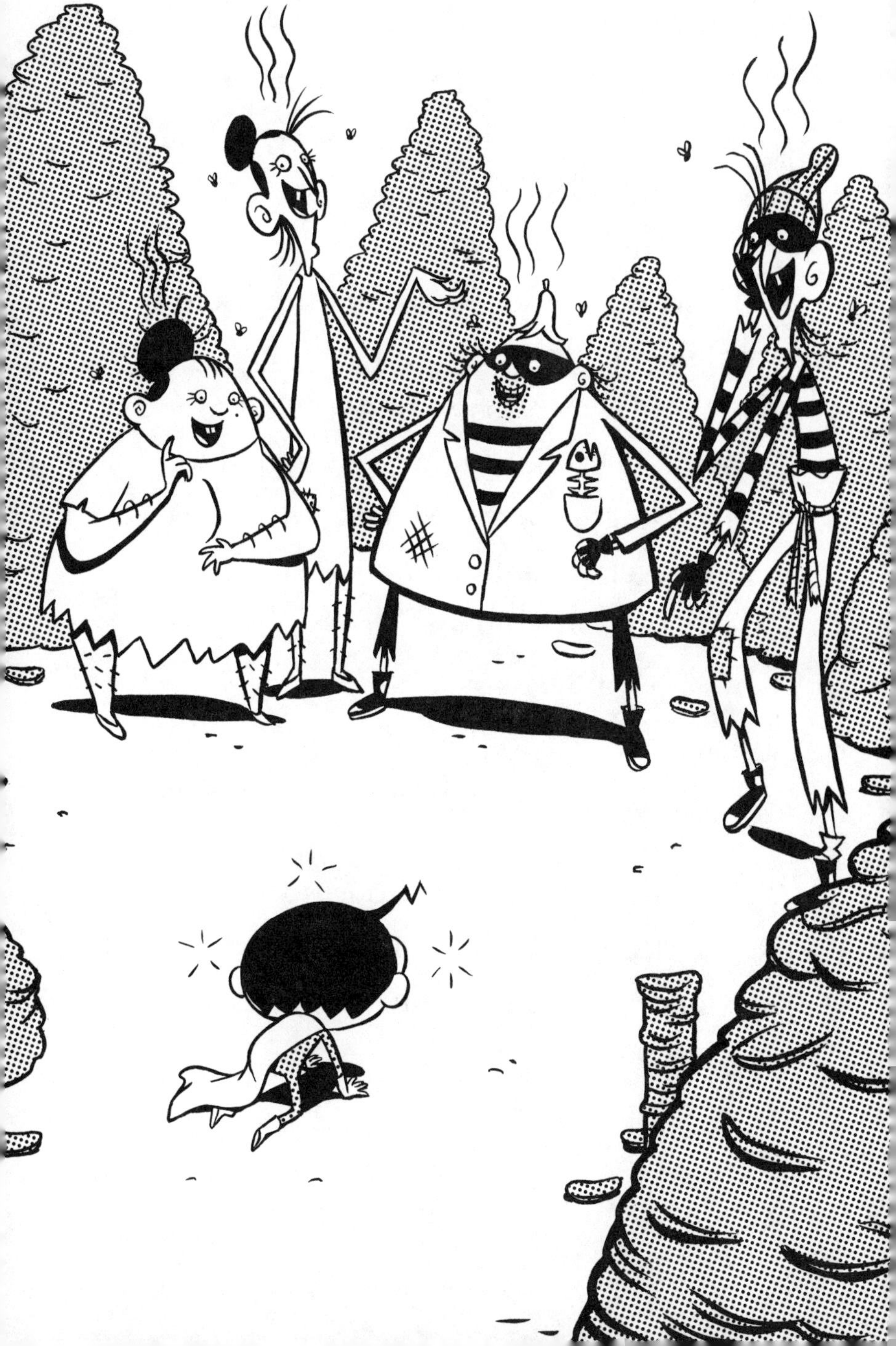

all-around bad girls? Anyway, I thought I'd make the introductions . . . before you DIE."

Melvin pinched his nose and said in a high-pitched voice, "Nice to meet you."

Filthy McNasty tied Melvin to the same post that Candace was tied to.

"Don't worry," Melvin whispered to her over his shoulder.

"You have a plan?"

"Not really."

"What kind of noggin power is that?"

"Be patient, Candace. I'm waiting for it to kick in."

"Stop that whispering," Grunge snarled. "Let me explain how this will work. Last time you escaped because you ate your way to freedom. That's not going to happen this time. Look around you." He gestured at the piles of lunch meat. "Six thousand pounds of bologna, ladies and gentlemen."

Mudball McNasty scanned the room. She didn't see a lady or a gentleman anywhere.

"I meant you guys," Grunge said.

"Yes. Of course. Exactly."

"As I was saying," Grunge continued, "there's no way out this time, Mister Melvin Beederman and Miss Candace Brinkwater. No one can eat six thousand pounds of bologna. No one. Not even a superhero."

Grunge held up a weird contraption made out of wires and what looked like a clock. "I've set the timer for three hours. Time enough for us to make our getaway and for the striking workers to head home. There'll be nobody left when the explosion happens. Six thousand pounds of bologna will go bye-bye. And so will you two."

Melvin sat with his head down. He knew Grunge was right. This time there was no way out.

MISSION IMPOSSIBLE

All afternoon Melvin Beederman and Candace Brinkwater struggled with the ropes that tied them to the post. All afternoon they grew weaker from the six thousand pounds of bologna. And all afternoon they heard the ticking of the time bomb, getting closer and closer to blowing up.

The McNasty Brothers and Sisters had long since made their getaway. The striking workers had gone home.

"Noggin power kicking in yet?" Candace asked, tugging at the ropes.

"Still thinking," Melvin replied.

He felt himself growing weaker by the minute, but fortunately bologna only affected his body. His brain was free to work.

"Work, brain, work," Melvin said out loud.

"Yes, work, Melvin's brain, work," Candace agreed.

Melvin thought through the Superhero's Code. What did it say about times like this?

Nothing, that's what.

The only part that might apply was "Your brain is your greatest weapon."

Only right now Melvin's brain didn't seem to be a weapon at all.

Tick tick tick.

They were running out of time.

Tick tick tick.

It was now or never.

All at once they heard a small noise in the corner of the room. Maybe they weren't as alone as they had thought!

"Hello?" Melvin called.

"Who's there?" Candace added.

The sound came again—a faint rustling—then tiny footsteps.

"Who's there?" Candace asked again.

The tiny footsteps stopped, then, "Squeak squeak."

"It's a rat!" Melvin said.

"Quick. Adopt it!"

"I already have a rat," Melvin said.

"Not for you. For me."

"No time for that. We need to get out

111

of here." But Melvin suddenly found himself thinking of his rat Hugo. It was nice to have a roommate. Someone to watch *The Adventures of Thunderman* with. Someone to drink root beer with. Someone to eat pret—

He had an idea. "Can you reach my back pocket, Candace?" They were tied to the post back-to-back.

"I think so. What am I looking for?"

"Pretzels. I keep snacks with me at all times."

Candace carefully reached into Melvin's pocket. "Got it," she said.

"Great!" Melvin turned to the rat and said, "Squeakity squeak."

The rat did nothing. Not even a twitch of its whiskers.

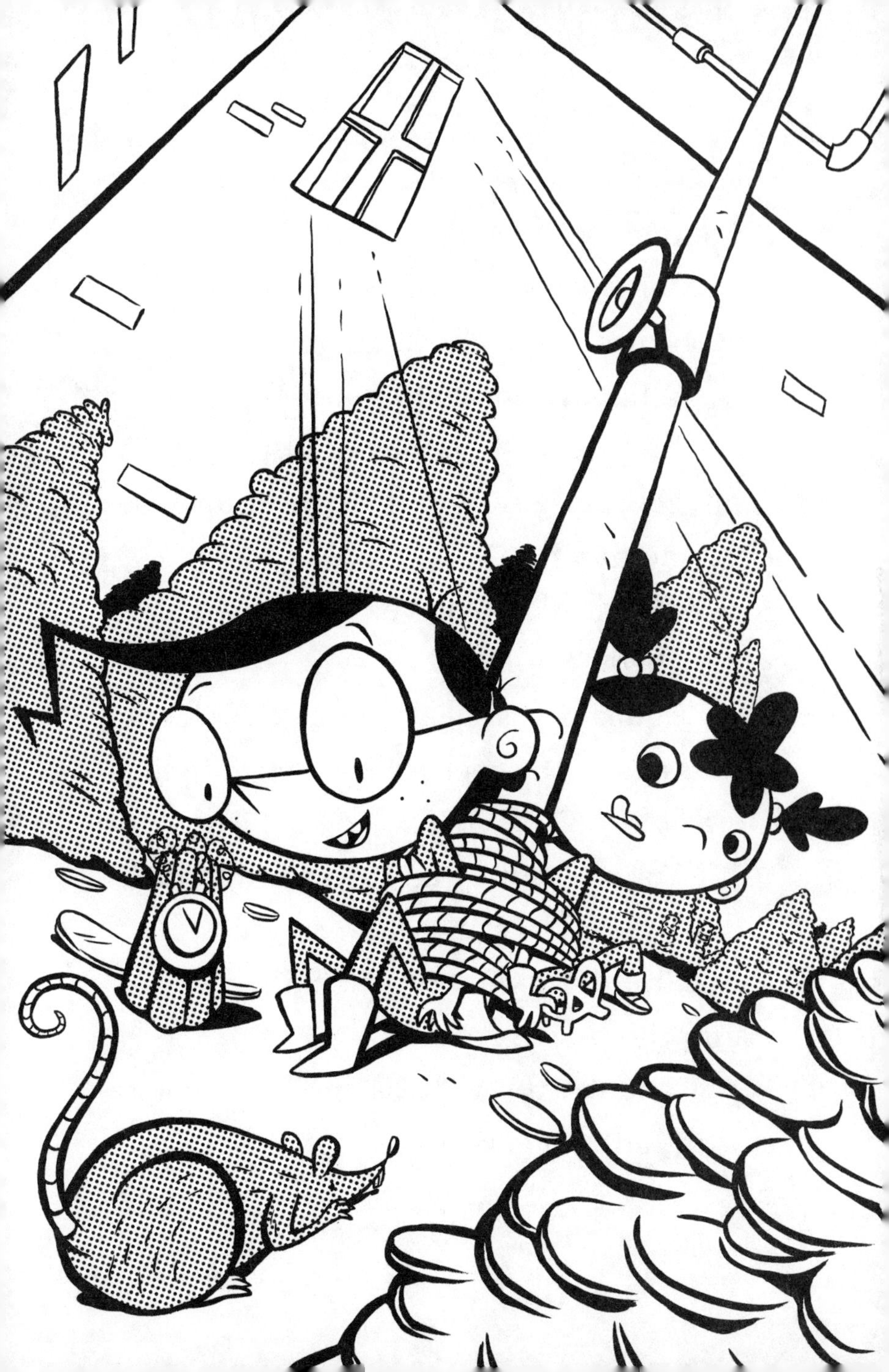

"Get those eyebrows going, Melvin," Candace suggested.

Melvin tried again, this time using his eyebrows. "Squeakity squeak squeak."

"What are you telling him?"

"I either said, 'How would you like a pretzel, big guy?' or, 'Do you know the way to San Jose?'"

The rat didn't move. Then a whisker twitched. "Squeak?"

"Squeakity squeak squeak?" Melvin said again. His eyebrows were going like crazy.

"You've got that eyebrow thing down," Candace said admiringly.

"Shhh. I think it's working. Throw him the pretzel."

Candace threw it as best she could with her hands tied.

The rat came forward and ate it quickly. "Squeak?"

"It wants more," Candace said.

"First things first." Melvin wiggled his eyebrows. "Squeak."

"What did you say?"

"I said, 'Chew through these ropes and we'll give you another pretzel.' At least I think that's what I said. Unless it was 'Do you know a truck driver named Fred?'"

The rat slowly came closer.

"No more treats until these ropes are off," Melvin said.

"Right."

The rat sniffed the ropes, then began to chew. Soon the two superheroes were free. Melvin dropped a few pretzels on the ground and squeaked a thank-you.

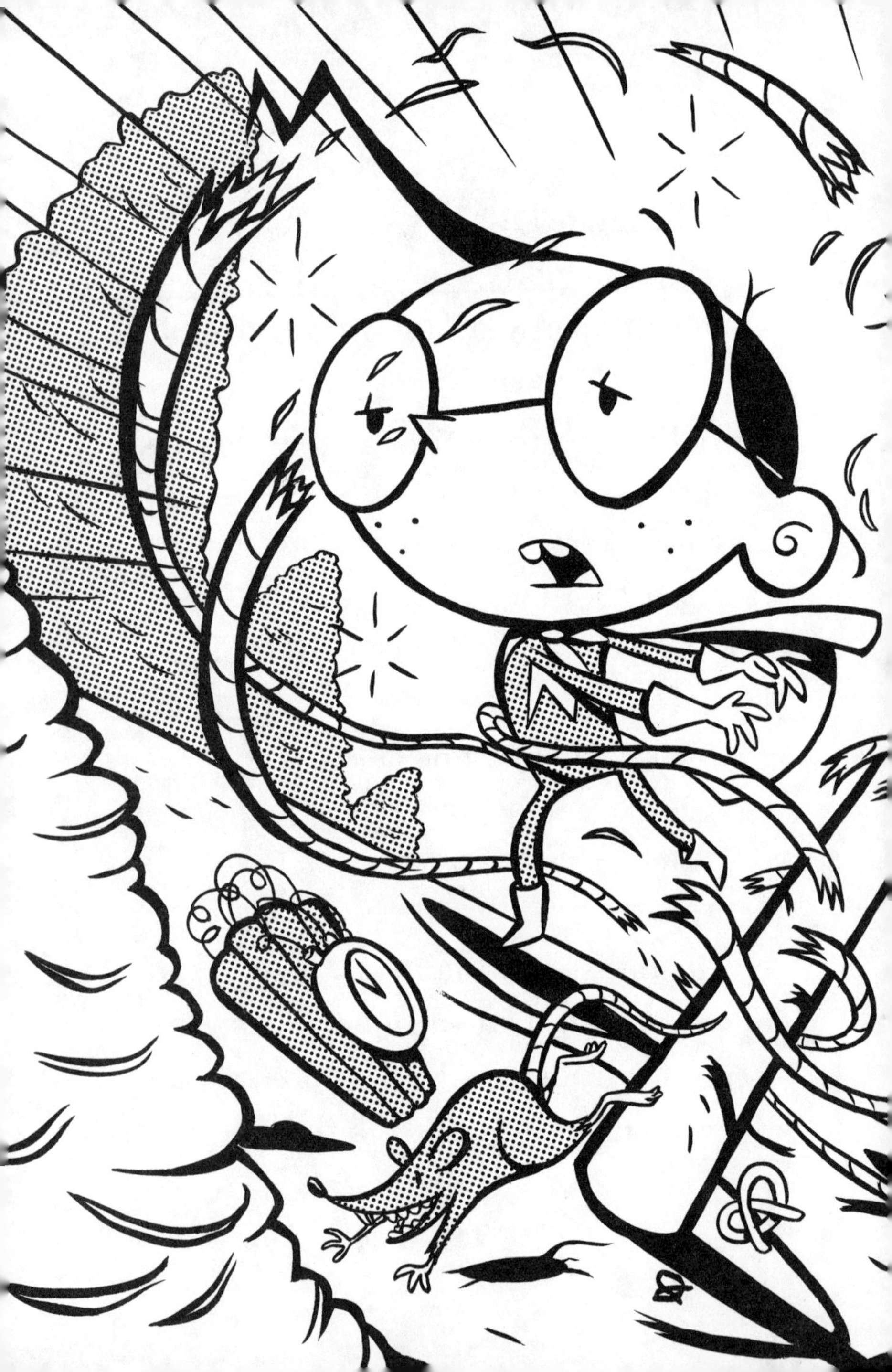

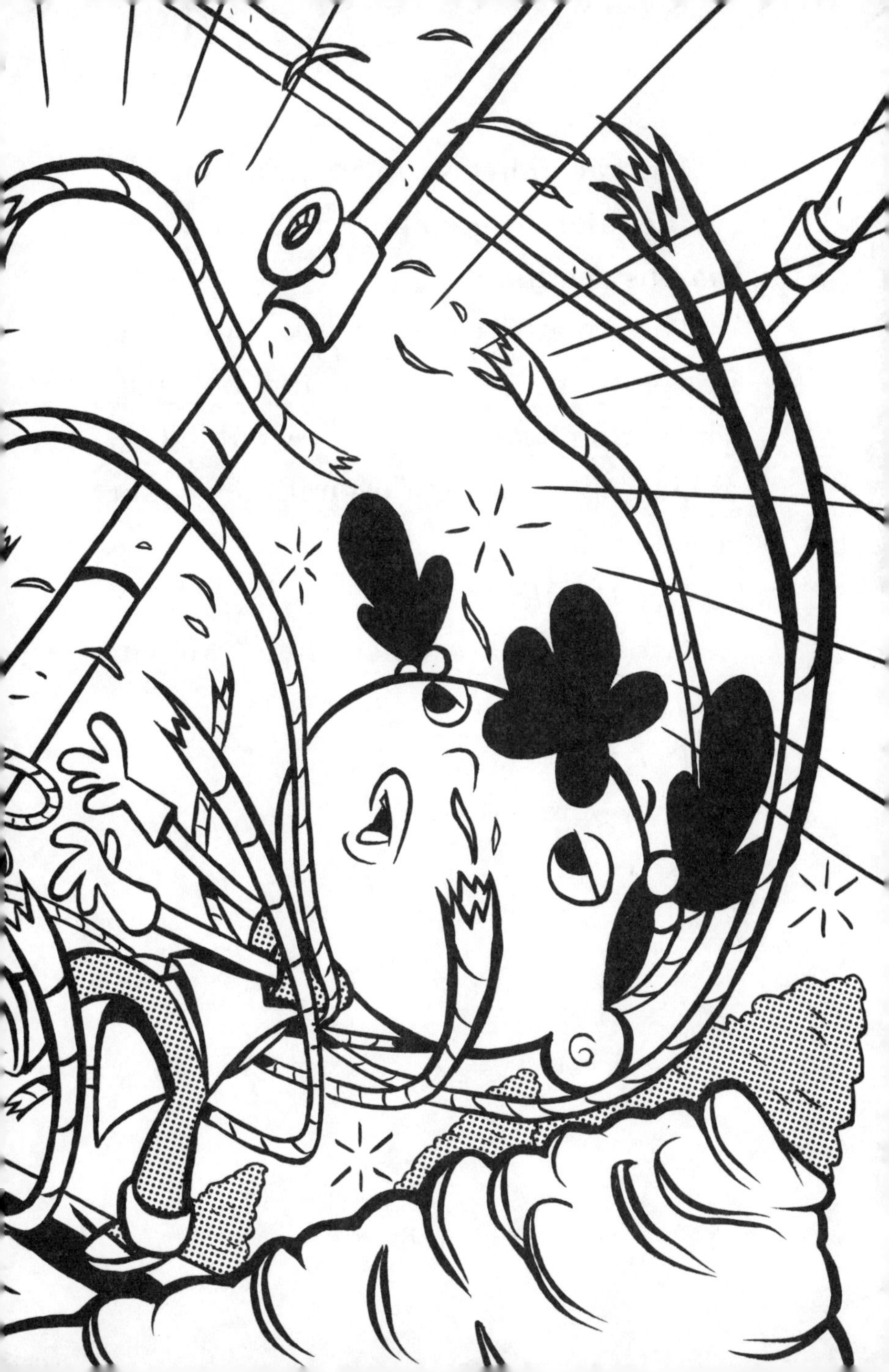

The rat didn't seem to care that his rescue efforts were appreciated. He was too busy eating.

The superheroes were free. But there was still the problem of the bologna. They had no strength. They wouldn't be able to open the door even if they could reach it.

Tick tick tick.

"We don't have much time," Melvin said.

Tick tick tick.

They sure didn't.

BOLOGNA PROBLEMS

"How do you feel?" Melvin asked his assistant.

"Can't . . . move . . . get . . . me . . . out . . . of . . . here. That pretty much sums it up."

Melvin looked around the warehouse. He saw huge containers of bologna and not much else.

Then he spotted something.

"Candace, when does kryptonite not affect Superman?" Melvin asked.

"Is this Twenty Questions? Because I'd much rather escape. Hear that ticking, Melvin? That's a bomb about to go off."

"Just answer the question."

"Okay, but then we need to get out of here or there won't be any more books in this series. Here's your answer: When kryptonite is enclosed in lead it doesn't affect Superman."

"Exactly," Melvin said. "Look over there, Candace." He pointed to a box a few feet away. "Look what's written on the box."

"Sandwich wrap?"

"Exactly. If we could somehow wrap ourselves in sandwich wrap, maybe it would protect us from the bologna. And we'd get our strength back."

"Melvin Beederman, your noggin power just showed up!"

Melvin nodded and crawled slowly toward the box of sandwich wrap. It took all his strength to get there. He opened the box and began wrapping himself in the stuff.

Now, shielded from the bologna, he stood up.

"Holy ridiculous-looking superhero!" Candace said.

Holy ridiculous-looking superhero, indeed! Melvin did look pretty silly covered in sandwich wrap. But now he had his strength back.

He walked over and wrapped Candace, too. She stood up.

"Do you know how to deactivate that bomb?" Melvin asked.

"Deactivate schmactivate." She walked over and one-punched the time bomb. It shattered into pieces, and the ticking stopped.

"Way to schmactivate," Melvin said. "Let's go get the bad guys."

Once outside, they unwrapped them-selves and took off.

Or at least Candace did.

"Be with you in a minute," Melvin said. "Up, up, and away."

Crash!

Splat!

Thud!

Kabonk!

Melvin Beederman joined Candace Brinkwater in the air on the fifth try, and they zoomed off together. Right then he realized something. He only got off the ground on the first try when his partner in uncrime was in trouble. That was okay by him. It wasn't part of the code, but Melvin knew it was a good idea to always look out for your partner.

THE McNASTYS MAKE THEIR GETAWAY . . . OR DO THEY?

"Where's the McNastys' hideout?" Melvin asked. They zoomed between the tall buildings of the city. Now that Candace was safe, Melvin stopped to flex at his reflection in the many windows.

"Follow me," Candace said. "But it's not a hideout—it's a lair."

The McNasty lair was built into the side of the hill below the Hollywood sign. *Nice lair*, Melvin thought as he kicked in

124

the door. Ever since his rescue attempt at the Acme Bologna Company he had been wanting to do that. And it felt good.

"That felt good," he said to Candace.

"I get the next one." Candace loved kicking in doors, too. It was a job perk.

They made their way to the living area of the lair and found it empty. No McNastys.

"Smells like vittles," Melvin said (not food—vittles).

"And tea," Candace said.

"They haven't been gone long, though. I can still smell something nasty."

Melvin and Candace heard a car start outside. They ran to the doorway. A minivan was speeding down the winding road beneath the Hollywood sign.

"The McNastys!"

Candace launched herself immediately. "No time to lose, Melvin."

"I'm not flying on this one. Get that minivan. I'll meet you there." Melvin wasn't faster than a speeding bullet for nothing. He was pretty sure he could run as fast as Candace could fly. And he did. She flew and he ran.

They plopped themselves in front of the minivan and stopped it dead in its tracks. "Come out with your hands up," Candace said.

Melvin elbowed her and whispered something.

"I mean, not so fast!" Then she looked at Melvin and smiled. "Better?"

"Exceedingly."

The doors to the minivan flew open.

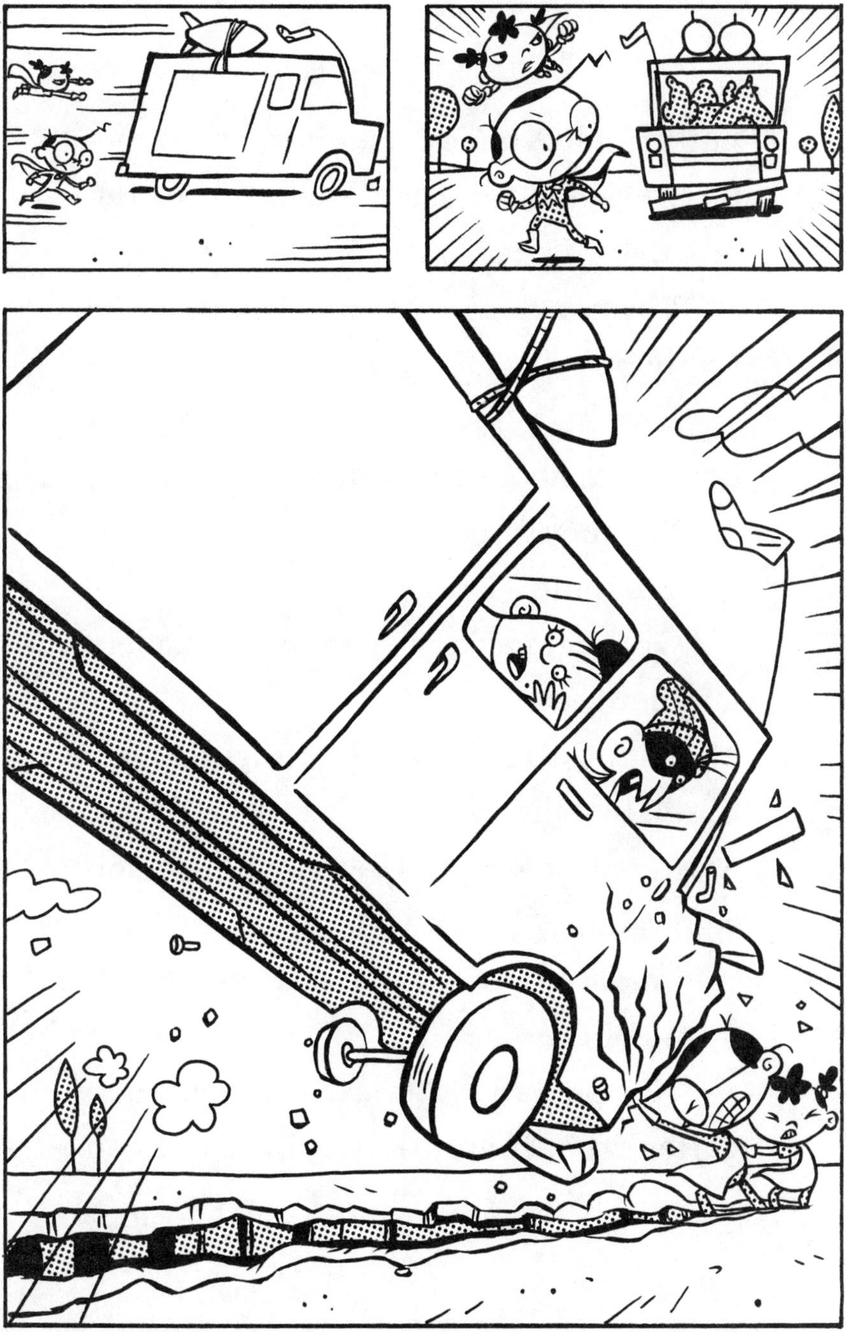

Filthy and Grunge took off in one direction; Mudball and Puke took off in the other.

"I can get the sisters. You get the brothers," Candace said.

"Just help me with the brothers. I don't care about the sisters."

"But they're getting away."

"Trust me, Candace."

"Oh, I get it. They might come back in another book?"

"Shhh." Melvin held a finger to his lips. Then he winked. "Let's get those McNasty Brothers. They have a prison cell waiting for them."

Candace flew.

Melvin ran.

"Not so fast!" At last Candace had gotten the lingo right. She grabbed

Filthy McNasty while Melvin took care
of the ringleader, Grunge McNasty . . .
and sent those notorious bank robbers
and all-around bad guys back to prison
where they belonged.

Later that day, the two superheroes were flying high over the city, discussing their adventure—the McNastys, the Acme Bologna Company, the lair (not hideout—lair).

They were so busy talking that they weren't paying attention to anything else.

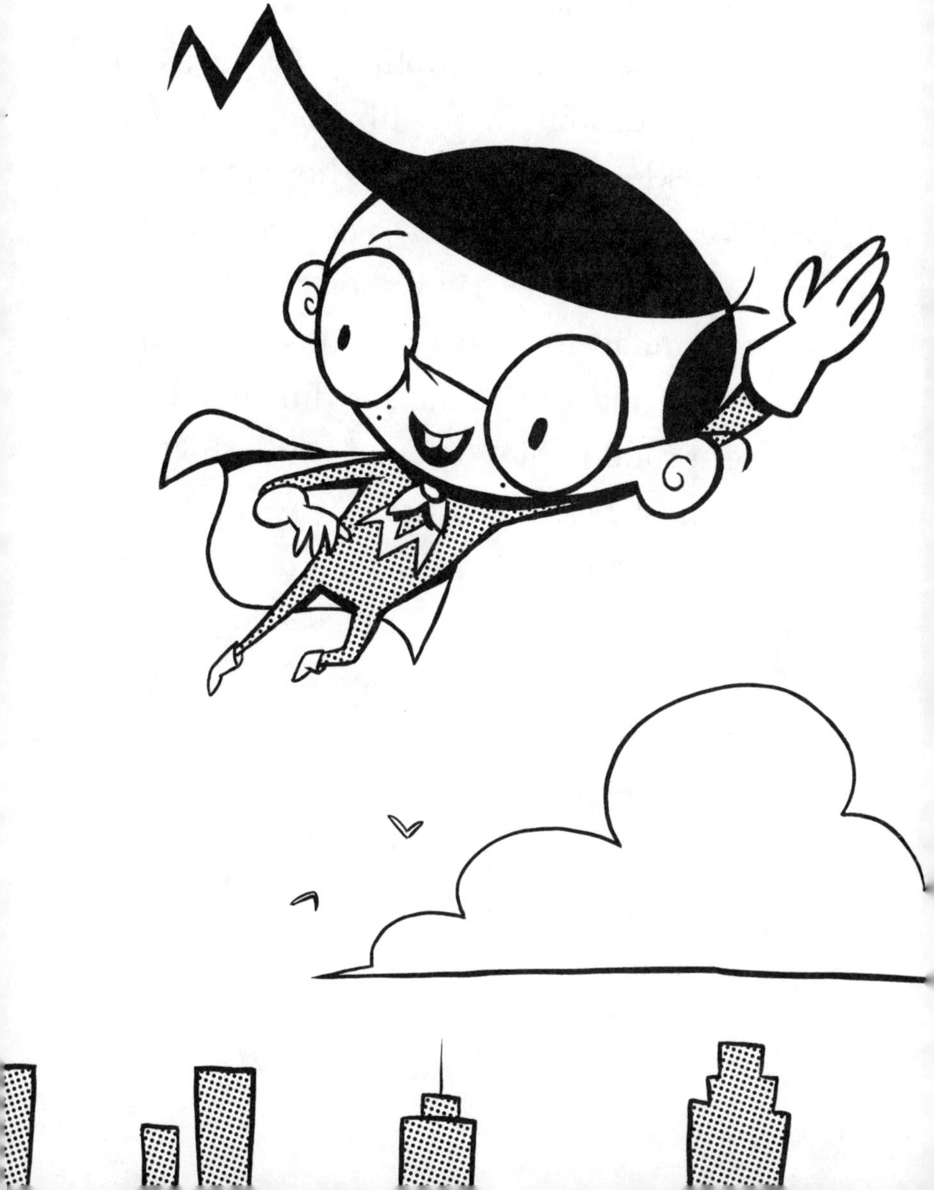

Things were quiet, which of course meant trouble was brewing.

Far below them, Johnny Fink was in his bedroom with his best friend, Knucklehead Wilson. They chanted, "We hate Brinkwater, yes, we do. We hate Brinkwater. How about you?"

Candace Brinkwater didn't hear this.

She made it home for dinner, where her proud family listened while she told them of her adventures. It was nice to have a daughter who saved the world on a regular basis.

After seeing Candace home, Melvin returned to his tree house. His pet rat Hugo was there waiting for him.

"Squeakity squeak squeak squeak," Melvin said with just the right amount of eyebrow wiggle. He thought he'd just said, "Would you care to watch *The Adventures of Thunderman*?" Or possibly it was "Do my feet stink?"

They did, but that's another story.

THE McNASTY CRIME SYNDICATE

FILTHY McNASTY

* What he loves: Loot (not money—loot)
* Fun fact: Has a pet turtle named Geraldine
* Favorite hobby: Collecting rubber bands in his spare time
* What he fears most: Bathing

GRUNGE McNASTY

* What he loves: Smelling bad
* What he hates: All superheroes, especially Melvin Beederman
* Favorite hobby: Cat juggling
* Claim to unfame: Was once awarded Worst-Smelling Bad Guy of the Year

MUDBALL McNASTY

* Fun fact: Left school in third grade
* Favorite hobby: Singing Grateful Fred songs in the shower
* What she hates: Taking orders from her sister Puke
* Claim to unfame: Got honorable mention in Worst-Smelling Bad Guy of the Year contest

PUKE McNASTY

* What she loves: Giving orders to her sister
* What she hates: Vegetables and superheroes
* Favorite hobby: Telling her sister to stop singing in the shower
* Claim to unfame: Made it past the third grade

135

THE DELETED SCENES

"Hey, Filthy, what's this doohickey with the clock?"

"Way to schmactivate!"

"Look, up in the sky, it's a . . . Buick?"

Coming soon! Melvin and Candace and
some guys named Fred in

THE GRATEFUL FRED

From: grateful@fred.fred
To: melvin@melvinbeederman.com

Dear Melvin,
We need your help. Someone has been sending us threatening letters. We don't know who it is. Please come to our concert tonight, just in case.

Sincerely,
Fred of The Grateful Fred